"Thanks for ma... today," Lily said with a smile.

"No problem," Mike responded. "Sorry it wasn't much of a riding lesson."

The sweet smile warmed to something he didn't quite understand. And wasn't sure he wanted to.

"Actually, I learned a lot. About you."

"Yeah? Like what?" he asked.

"That you don't hesitate to put yourself in danger to help an animal when it's in trouble. That says a lot about a person, don't you think?"

"I guess so," he hedged, feeling awkward and proud at the same time. He wasn't used to being praised for simply being himself.

"Someone like that is just the person I want teaching me. Do you think you can work me into your schedule again soon?"

"How 'bout Monday at four?" he heard himself ask, cringing at the eager tone in his voice.

Since he couldn't take it back, he did his best to act as if seeing her again that soon didn't matter all that much one way or the other. When deep down, he knew it did matter. A lot.

Mia Ross loves great stories. She enjoys reading about fascinating people, long-ago times and exotic places. But only for a little while, because her reality is pretty sweet. Married to her college sweetheart, she's the proud mom of two amazing kids, whose schedules keep her hopping. Busy as she is, she can't imagine trading her life for anyone else's—and she has a pretty good imagination. You can visit her online at miaross.com.

Books by Mia Ross

Love Inspired

Oaks Crossing

Her Small-Town Cowboy

Barrett's Mill

Blue Ridge Reunion
Sugar Plum Season
Finding His Way Home
Loving the Country Boy

Holiday Harbor

Rocky Coast Romance
Jingle Bell Romance
Seaside Romance

Hometown Family
Circle of Family
A Gift of Family
A Place for Family

Her Small-Town Cowboy

Mia Ross

Recycling programs for this product may not exist in your area.

 LOVE INSPIRED BOOKS

ISBN-13: 978-0-373-81885-3

Her Small-Town Cowboy

www.Harlequin.com

Printed in U.S.A.

Forgive, and you will be forgiven.
—*Luke* 6:37

For Ruth

Acknowledgments

To the very talented folks who help me
make my books everything they can be:
Elaine Spencer, Melissa Endlich
and the dedicated staff at Love Inspired.

More thanks to the gang at Seekerville
(www.seekerville.net), a great place
to hang out with readers—and writers.

I've been blessed with a wonderful network of
supportive, encouraging family and friends.
You inspire me every day!

Chapter One

Mike Kinley hated weddings.

Maybe *hate* was a little strong, he amended as he guided a team of perfectly matched bays into the shade of a nearby oak tree. Setting the carriage's brake with his boot, he glanced over at the gazebo where a photographer was taking shots of the bride and groom he'd just delivered. *Poor kids,* Mike thought with a grimace. They had no idea what they were in for.

Then again, neither had he. He'd done everything in his power to make Dana happy, and where did that get him? Divorced and wishing he'd listened to his head instead of his heart. Now he was thirty years old and working seven days a week desperately trying to hold up his end of a faltering family business. If they couldn't come up with a way to bring in more cash—and soon—their shaky bottom line would crater to a depth they wouldn't be able to recover from. They'd be forced to sell the place that generations of Kinleys had worked so hard to build up from a scenic blue-grass meadow to the well-respected Gallimore Stables. He and his brothers would be hunting for jobs, and his mother would lose the home she cherished so much. While Mike couldn't deny that weddings brought in some much-needed revenue, they sure were tough on his nerves.

And seeing as it was early May in Kentucky, wedding season had only begun.

Hoping to get himself back to his usual even keel, he jumped down and took a small tackle box from the well where he rested his feet when he was driving. Taking out a soft cloth and brush, he began rubbing the horses down, talking as much to entertain himself as them.

"There's my girl, Penny," he cooed in a quiet voice. "We'll get you shined up, and then it's your turn, Ginger. Folks'll want to pet you later on, so you've gotta be looking your best."

Breaking his own strict rule about not feeding the horses, he slipped a hand into the pocket of the elegant morning coat his sister forced him to wear for these gigs and brought out a few sugar cubes for each of them. After they slurped down their treats, he ran his hands down their legs in a practiced motion, lifting their hooves to make sure no gravel from the estate's pathways had gotten wedged into their shoes.

Satisfied that everything was okay, he stood between them and patted their outside shoulders. "Lookin' good, ladies."

In unison, the beautiful mares tossed their heads and whinnied back at him. Behind him, he heard a woman laugh. Careful not to startle the horses, he slowly turned to find a slender bridesmaid coming down the wide steps that led out to the gardens from one of the three reception halls. Wearing a pale blue dress that looked as if it was made of spun sugar, she seemed right at home in her elegant surroundings. A few curls had escaped her elaborate hairdo, framing a pair of sparkling eyes that were nearly the same color as her dress. His poetic reaction to her was totally unlike him, and he sternly reminded himself to keep things professional.

"If I didn't know better," she commented in a melodic drawl, "I'd think they understood what you said to them."

"Oh, they did. They're female, so they can never get enough compliments." Even to his ears, that came across as jaded, and he tried to soften the impact by extending his hand. "Mike Kinley, carriage driver."

After a moment, she gave him a shy smile and shook his hand. "Lily St. George, runaway bridesmaid."

That was a new one, he mused with more than a little curiosity. Normally, he wouldn't even think of asking her to explain. But he had at least an hour to kill while he waited for his passengers, and although he thought horses made great companions, they weren't much in the conversation department. "Mind if I ask why?"

"My younger sister is the bride, which is wonderful." Pausing, she frowned. "The groom is my ex-boyfriend."

"Not so wonderful." When she sighed and nodded, the sadness that came into her eyes brought back some of the mood he'd been trying to shed. Thanks to Dana, he knew how it felt to be cast aside and then discover how easily you'd been replaced. So, even though he knew it was probably something he'd end up regretting, he offered her a solution. "The ceremony's over, right? You could just leave."

"My whole family's in there, so I can't do that. What would everyone think?"

That it was cruel to ask you to be part of your ex's wedding party? Catching himself before he insulted this sweet stranger, he searched for a way to lift her spirits. He noticed her eyeing the horses, and inspiration hit. "Would you like a tour of the grounds?"

"In the carriage?" When he nodded, her eyes rounded with excitement. "I'd love to, but are you sure it's okay? I mean, you're working another wedding."

"We're waiting for them to finish their pictures," he replied with a nod toward the large group, "and the horses get antsy when they stand still for too long. We were headed out for a walk and some water, anyway."

Technically, that was true, even if he hadn't been planning to go just yet. For this time of year, the day wasn't all that warm, so he figured the extra circuit wouldn't do the horses any harm. While he didn't normally put himself out for wedding guests this way, the delight shining in Lily's eyes told him he'd made the right decision to make an exception for her.

As he prepared to hand her up into the tufted velvet passenger section of the carriage, she hesitated for some reason. "Is something wrong?"

Casting a longing look at the padded driver's seat, she turned those stunning baby blues on him. "Could I ride up front with you?"

"Most folks like the royal treatment."

A flicker of disapproval flashed across her face, and she firmly shook her head. "Not me. Besides, if I sit in back, we can't talk to each other."

That had been part of his plan, Mike admitted to himself reluctantly. Harsh experience had taught him not to trust anyone—especially anyone female—too easily. His tried-and-true strategy was to keep people at a safe distance until he could be sure they were who they seemed to be. Because of that, he didn't have a lot of friends, and the ones with the integrity and fortitude to get through his defenses were there to stay.

"I'm not much of a talker," he hedged, hoping to dissuade her without being outright rude.

"That's okay," she replied brightly. "I am. And I'd love to sit up near the horses, if they won't mind."

Her concern for the mares' preference settled it for him. Anyone who considered the feelings of animals was on the way to being all right in his book. "Let's ask 'em. Whattya think, girls?"

Right on cue, Penny nodded her approval while Ginger let out a muted whinny. Laughing, his passenger said, "I think they like me."

Who wouldn't? Mike nearly blurted. Firmly

shoving the errant thought aside, he bowed the way his sister insisted he do and politely handed Lily up to the wide bench driver's seat. Then he circled around the carriage and settled in beside her. As he picked up the reins, it occurred to him that he probably wasn't the first guy to go out of his way for her. "Just so I don't end up in trouble, are you here with anyone?"

"No." The light in her eyes dimmed, but she quickly recovered and gave him what was obviously a determined smile. "I'm alone."

Her resigned tone made him want to do something about that, and he cautioned himself not to follow that crazy impulse. *Romantic nonsense,* he reasoned, brought on by the tenth wedding he'd worked in the past month. Even a pragmatist like him could take only so much sentiment before he was tempted to ignore his better judgment and join in the insanity.

In the interest of keeping things between them as light as possible, he gave her a quick grin. "Not anymore. The Marbury Estate is one of the oldest in Kentucky whose original main house and grounds are still intact. What would you like to see first?"

"Everything."

"You heard her, girls." He clucked to the gleaming mares. "Let's get a move on."

As they started off in an easy trot, Lily said,

"When they move, it's like brown silk floating over the ground. They're so beautiful."

A woman after his own heart, he realized with a mental sigh. This little tour was either the best idea he'd ever had, or the worst. Then again, afterward they'd part ways and never see each other again, so he figured there was no harm in being nice.

"So," he began in his best conversational tone, "where are you from?"

For some reason, she held back for a moment, then seemed to decide it was all right to share her hometown with him. "Louisville."

After that, she looked around the manicured park, at the horses, the stately oaks arching overhead, anywhere but at him. He couldn't imagine what all the avoidance was about, but he reminded himself that women were complex creatures no man in his right mind would even pretend to understand. The runaway bridesmaid had a right to her secrets, especially since her personal history was absolutely none of his business.

Looping onto a path that wound through the rose garden, he switched to a lighter topic. "What do you do?"

Immediately, her mood brightened, and the smile that lit her face nearly knocked him sideways. "Actually, I just got my first teaching job. I'll be filling in for a kindergarten teacher for the rest of the school year while she's out on maternity leave."

"Hope it goes well for you."

"So do I," Lily agreed in a tentative voice. "It's my first assignment since getting my degree, and I have to admit I'm a little nervous about taking over a class this way. Young kids get really attached to their teachers, and I'm hoping they'll give me a chance."

Mike couldn't picture anyone not taking to Lily right out of the gate, but he opted not to mention that. "You're bigger than them. How tough can they be?"

"You have no idea."

He wasn't quite sure what to say, and he searched his limited social repertoire for some encouraging words. When he recalled how Mom used to handle the passel of kids always roaming around the farm, he offered, "If things get too bad, you can always bribe 'em with cookies. Works with me, too."

What had possessed him to add that last comment? This pretty teacher couldn't care less about whether he enjoyed snacks or not. Fortunately, either she didn't notice his misstep, or she was incredibly forgiving.

"Cookies," she echoed with a little grin. "I'll

keep that in mind. Do you have any other suggestions for me?"

He answered with the kind of laugh that was pretty rare for him these days. "Not hardly."

"But you know children like cookies. That's a start."

"Everyone does," he said, giving her a sidelong glance as he guided the team around a sweeping curve in the path.

She rewarded his uncharacteristic helpfulness with the most incredible smile he'd ever seen in his life. As he felt himself returning the friendly gesture, inwardly Mike groaned.

It was a good thing she lived in Louisville. His gut was usually bang on about people, and it was telling him that Lily St. George had the potential to cause him no end of trouble.

Calling Mike Kinley an interesting man would be the understatement of the year.

To Lily's great relief, he hadn't reacted to her name the way most people did when she first met them. That was just the way she wanted it, since she despised having to be pleasant to people who were clearly more interested in her wealthy, connected family than in her. She couldn't recall how many times supposed friends had asked her for an introduction at one of the many companies her family owned, only to ditch her once they had what they wanted. Finally, in college she'd had the opportunity to start over with a fresh batch of friends who had no clue about her privileged background. She'd confided the truth to a select few, but only after she was confident they'd bonded with her and not her family's money.

Mike took her on a leisurely tour of the estate's breathtaking grounds, and she gradually relaxed as they chatted off and on about nothing in particular. While he concentrated on the horses, she took advantage of the opportunity to study him more closely. Being female, she couldn't help admiring what she saw.

Any man would look dapper in the crisp white shirt and gray morning suit, but there was more to his appearance than that. Sun-streaked brown hair brushed his starched collar, telling her he spent a lot of time outdoors. His white gloves rested on the seat between them, and she saw that his large hands were calloused from plenty of hard work. The easy, confident way he held the reins spoke of a life-time spent around horses.

And then there were his eyes. A unique mix of blue and gray, they focused on her more directly than most people's did, as if he was listening intently to her. She didn't think she was being particularly entertaining, which made his attention even more flattering. Unlike most men she knew who went out of their way to compliment her appearance, this outdoorsy carriage driver actually seemed interested in what she had to say. It was a refreshing change.

As if that wasn't enough, he seemed to know everything about the antebellum estate, patiently answering her questions and pointing out various historical spots spread throughout the sprawling grounds. The house itself had been around since the early 1800s, surviving the ravages of the Civil War by serving as a headquarters for both Union and Confederate commanders. The well-tended gardens were breathtaking, filled with brilliant colors and bracketed by what looked to be miles of immaculately trimmed boxwood.

It was the ideal spot for a wedding, and she could understand why Natalie had chosen it. The husband she'd chosen to share that day with was another matter altogether, but Lily reminded herself it wasn't her place to question the decisions her younger sister made. Now that the wedding was over, Lily's only job was to support the new couple.

Unfortunately, her less-than-stellar experience with Chad made her fear that the freshly minted Mrs. Wellington was going to need all the love and understanding she could get.

"This is such a pretty spot," Lily commented while they drove beneath a grove of oaks draped in Spanish moss. Nearby stood the mansion with its wide front steps, where her sister's photographer had snapped dozens of pictures for the wedding album. "I wonder how many people have been married here over the years."

"A few."

His tone struck her as being overly polite, and she laughed. "Sorry about that. You must have heard that about a million times."

"A few," he repeated with a wry grin. Pulling gently on the reins, he stopped the horses near a small creek that wound its way through the picturesque clearing in the trees. "If you don't mind stopping here for a few minutes, the girls could use a drink."

"I don't mind a bit. Would it be all right if I pet them while they're drinking?"

He climbed down and gave her a dubious once-over. "You want to handle horses dressed like that?"

"Trust me—your horses are a lot cleaner than the best man's toast was."

Mike laughed, then held up a hand for her to take. The old-fashioned gesture seemed ideally suited to this fairy-tale setting, and she felt like a princess when she landed on the ground beside him. Her heels sank into the soft soil, and rather than ruin the dyed satin shoes, she stepped out of them onto the velvety grass.

Squishing her toes into it, she sighed. "That's the best my feet have felt all day."

"Interesting look," he teased with a grin. "And here I am without my camera."

Before she knew what she was doing, she'd stuck her tongue out at him. It was so unlike her, she felt her face reddening with embarrassment. "Mike, I'm sorry. That was rude of me."

"No need to apologize. I thought it was funny."

He gave her a long, pensive look before turning away to unhitch the horses. While she watched him, Lily tried desperately to regain her usual equilibrium. Raised to anticipate any social situation that might crop up, she wasn't prone to being surprised out of her well-schooled habits. Somehow, this man, with his windblown good looks and down-to-earth nature, had thoroughly rattled her without even seeming to try.

She wasn't sure how he'd managed it, but fortunately she wouldn't have to worry about running into him in the future. They were from completely different worlds, and their paths weren't likely to ever cross again. That knowledge should have made her feel better about her bizarre response to him.

In all honesty, it only made her wonder what she'd be missing.

When one of the horses splashed some water out of the creek and onto Mike's polished black boots, he chuckled. "Guess they're done. Ready to go back?"

"Not really." Gazing toward the grand reception hall, she sighed, then looked back at him and forced a smile. "But I probably should. I've taken up enough of your time already."

"Wasn't going anywhere in particular," he assured her in an easygoing drawl. "Like I said, the girls needed a lap around, anyway. I appreciated having some company."

"Really? You're not just saying that to be nice?"

"I never say anything just to be nice," he informed her curtly. But there was a mischievous twinkle in his eyes, and she laughed as he gave a little bow and helped her back into her seat. She couldn't tell if the gruff demeanor was his true personality, or if the brief glimpses of humor she'd gotten were more him. Instinct told her he was a blend of the two, which made him the most intriguing person she'd met in a long time.

Their trip back was much quicker than the

one out. Before she knew it, she was standing outside the hall, listening while the DJ talked her sister's guests through the steps of the latest line dance.

Turning to Mike, she managed to put aside her misgivings and smile. "Thanks for rescuing me for a little while."

"No problem." Tilting his head, he gave her a worried look. "You gonna be okay?"

"Sure. This thing can't last forever, and I've been through worse days."

That got her a suspicious look. "Yeah? When?"

There was the day she informed her family she wanted to drop her art classes and become a teacher. They simply didn't understand why anyone would choose a career she didn't technically need. But she'd stood her ground, and in the end her independence had won out. So far, anyway. That wasn't the kind of thing she'd share with a stranger, of course, so she kept it to herself.

"None recently that I can recall," she confessed, "but I'm sure there's been at least one."

"So you're an optimist."

There was a distinct growl to his tone, and she frowned. "You make that sound like a bad thing."

"Works for some folks, I guess." His dismissive shrug made it clear what he thought of them, though.

"But not for you?"

"Not hardly."

She nearly asked him to explain, but his tightened jaw warned her that would be a very bad idea. Determined to make the best of a suddenly awkward situation, she said, "It was great meeting you, Mike. Thanks again for the ride."

"You're welcome. I hope everything works out for your sister."

"Me, too."

She stepped away as he climbed into the carriage and clucked to the bays before heading toward the gazebo. From this angle, she noticed the subtle gold lettering that arched along the back of the carriage: Gallimore Stables. The poetic name seemed very much at odds with his temperament, and she wondered who'd chosen it. Watching until they disappeared around a bend in the road, she mulled over their unusual meeting. Mike was by far the most puzzling man she'd ever met, by turns thoughtful and brusque. Still, no one could miss the fondness he felt for Penny and Ginger, and that made her suspect there was more going on with him than met the eye. A lot more.

It was just as well they were going their separate ways, she decided as she squared her shoulders and turned to go inside. She'd shouldered other people's burdens before, and it had never ended well for her. Building a life for herself would take everything she could give it, and she had no intention of ever taking on someone else's baggage again.

For the time being, she had more than enough to worry about—like making it through the rest of this difficult day with a smile on her face.

Chapter Two

Monday morning, Lily got to work an hour earlier than was strictly necessary. She had the teacher's lesson plans for the remainder of the year tucked in her briefcase, but she didn't really need them. Eager to do a bang-up job in her first solo assignment, she'd memorized the material to be sure she understood everything.

Anything worth doing is worth doing to the hilt.

Her grandfather's voice echoed in her mind, and she paused a moment to smile at the memory. The advice had come with a generous check and a proud smile, as he told her to use the money for her exciting new life. Aside from him, her family and friends couldn't comprehend why teaching was so important to her, but she was determined to do something that would make a difference in the world. She couldn't imagine anything better than giving children a solid foundation to build the rest of their lives on.

Still smiling, she stowed her gear inside the modest wooden desk and took a moment to survey the bright, cheery kindergarten room. Small chairs were neatly clustered around four round tables, and she counted twenty seats. Which meant she had twenty students coming in soon for—she checked her color-coded schedule—show-and-tell.

Apparently, their veteran teacher had devised a simple and enjoyable way to make Lily's first day a little easier. Five kids were slated for the presentation, which would allow her to observe them without making anyone uncomfortable. Lily made a mental note to send the thoughtful woman a thank-you email later on.

The room was located in the front of the old brick building, and she watched as yellow buses started filing in to park diagonally in the lot. Students streamed out, laughing and yelling, while the teachers assigned to bus duty gathered them into groups to head inside. Fortunately, the principal had let Lily slide on that one. She wasn't proud to admit it, but she had a hunch that if her first day had begun with her facing a screaming horde of unfamiliar children, she might have bolted and never come back.

As it was, she wasn't sure where to stand while she waited for her class to arrive. Standing by her desk seemed stiff and formal, but the middle of the reading circle felt goofy to her. In the end, she settled for leaning against the open door wearing what she hoped came across as a welcoming smile. Her students started coming in, and she felt her confidence wavering as they brushed past her and went through what was clearly a well-ingrained morning routine.

Once they'd put everything away and settled in their seats, she checked the hallway to make sure there weren't any stragglers. Satisfied, she closed the door and turned to face the room full of fresh, curious faces.

"Good morning, everyone." Her voice sounded faint and strained, and she took a bracing breath before trying again. "I'm Miss St. George, and I'll be filling in for Mrs. Howard while she's out with her baby. I'll do my best to learn your names quickly, but there are a lot of you, so I hope you'll be patient with me."

A cute blonde girl with bright blue eyes and freckles quickly raised her hand. "Miss St. George?"

"Yes?"

"I'm Abby, and my daddy's here for show-and-tell." She pointed toward the window in the door. "Can I let him in?"

"Sure. Go ahead."

Abby sprang up to meet him, and Lily turned to say hello. Any thought of speaking left her mind when she saw that there, framed in the doorway, stood Mike Kinley. The formal gray suit had given way to jeans, a cowboy hat and a faded denim shirt with *Gallimore Stables* and a stylized horse head embroidered on the chest pocket. Being a woman, she had to admit this outfit suited him much better.

"Morning," he greeted her in the mellow drawl she thought she'd never hear again. Eyes twinkling in fun, he added a slight grin. "Thanks for having me in today."

Obviously, he didn't want his daughter to know he'd already met her new teacher. More than happy to pretend they'd never seen each other before, Lily played along. "Thanks for coming to spend some time with us." Turning, she noticed the kids gawking and couldn't help smiling. "From your reaction, I assume you all know Mr. Kinley."

Mike winced, and she couldn't figure out why until Abby clued her in. "I didn't tell you who he is yet. How do you know his name?"

"I'm on the visitors' list for today," he answered smoothly, giving Lily a nudging look. "That's how she knew."

Was he really? she wondered. She'd been so excited for her first day, she hadn't thought to do more than briefly check in at the office. She hated to start out by lying to her students, but since she didn't have any other brilliant ideas, she decided she had no option other than to allow his explanation to stand.

Thankfully, the overhead speakers crackled and a boy's trembling voice prompted them all to stand for the Pledge of Allegiance. The familiar phrases calmed Lily's nerves a bit, and in her head she kept repeating, "I can do this. I can do this."

She was keenly aware of Mike standing beside her, and while the children resettled in their seats, she couldn't help sneaking a peek or two at their guest. When he looked down at her, he gave her a subtle wink and the crooked grin that had charmed her during their carriage ride. When he wasn't growling about something, anyway.

She caught herself smiling back, then remembered where they were and quickly doused her response. But he'd noticed. The smirk he was wearing told her that much. He was probably one of those superobservant people who noticed everything that happened around him, she lamented with a sigh. Leave it to her to run across one of the last attentive males on the planet.

Anxious to move on, she clapped her hands to get the kids' attention. "All right, everyone, let's get in a circle on the story rug." Once they were more or less quiet, she motioned to Mike. "You're on."

A flash that struck her as mild panic passed over his sunburned features, but he quickly recovered and sat down. Not in the adult-sized teacher's chair she'd left open for him, she noticed with curiosity, but on the floor, cross-legged like the kids. Something about his desire to join them on their level made her smile. Maybe he wasn't as standoffish as she'd assumed.

He introduced himself as a horse trainer, then opened his palms and spread them apart. "What would you guys like to know?"

Small hands shot into the air, and he answered questions ranging from how much does a horse eat to how often he cleaned their stalls. He took each one with a serious expression, and his respect for the children impressed her. Then one little boy stopped their guest cold.

"Do you still miss your dad?"

Mike's patient smile froze in place, and he

seemed to pull back into himself. Clearly, the class knew their guest much better than she did, and in an effort to save him, Lily jumped in. "Does anyone have something they want to ask about the farm?"

"No, that's okay," Mike said quietly. Giving the boy an understanding look, he asked, "Did your father pass away?"

"Last year." Tears welled in his already large brown eyes, making them look even bigger. "I started baseball this year, and he'll never get to see me play."

Lily's heart lurched in sympathy, but she kept quiet. Mike had connected with this child in a way she could never manage, so she thought it best to let him handle the sensitive moment.

"What's your name, son?" he asked gently.

"Peter."

"Well, Peter, I know it's tough to lose your father, but you have to do your best to make him proud, even though he's not here to see it."

"How?"

"Do what you think he'd want you to, even if you'd rather be doing something else. Take good care of your mom 'cause she's missing him, too. Do you have brothers and sisters?"

"Two little sisters." Peter made a face. "They're such a pain."

Mike chuckled. "I hear you, but you're the oldest, so you've gotta watch out for them. When things get hard, families have to stick together."

"That's what Mom says."

"She's right. Even when you think she's not," he added with a wink. The boy laughed and nodded, then sank back into his spot with a satisfied look.

Mike fielded several more questions, and when the kids seemed to be getting restless, Lily decided it was time to let him go.

Standing, she moved in behind him. "I'm sure we all want to thank Mr. Kinley for coming in today." After a rousing chorus of appreciation, she held up her hands for quiet. "You have some seat work to do before our next visitor gets here. Please pick up where you left off on Friday."

They complied with only minimal grumbling, and she motioned Mike toward the door. He looked relieved to leave the inquisitive circle behind him.

"Man," he began in a hushed voice, "some of those kids are smarter than me."

"I feel awful that Peter brought up your father that way."

"It's not your fault." Gazing over at his daughter, he went on. "Dad died three years ago in a car accident, and it was big news around here. Abby doesn't really remember him, but she's heard us talk about him. I'm sure she's told her friends all the stories by now."

The misery clouding his eyes told Lily he was putting up a brave front to hide the sorrow he still felt over losing his dad. She adored her own father, and she couldn't begin to imagine how painful it would be to have him jerked out of her life that way. "I'm very sorry for your family's loss."

"Thanks."

The brusque response told her it was time to let the matter drop, so she moved on. "How are Penny and Ginger doing?"

"Just fine. And you? How was the rest of your sister's reception?"

Lily thought it was sweet of him to ask how that endless afternoon had affected her, even though she hadn't been the bride. Judging by the way his eyes were fixed on her, his concern was genuine, and she smiled. "It won't go in my favorite-memories list, but I made it through in one piece. I have to admit, I was kind of stunned to see you here this morning."

"I can relate to that," he admitted with a chuckle. "When Abby said her new teacher would be here, I had no clue it'd be you. You said you were from Louisville, so I figured that's where your school was."

"And I had no idea Gallimore Stables was here in Oaks Crossing."

"Yeah," he responded with a sigh. "That's a real problem for us. We're working on it, though."

"Really?" Leaning back against her desk, she eyed him with a new sense of respect. Apparently, the gruff carriage driver had more going for him than his rugged good looks. "How?"

"Dad trained Thoroughbreds for racing, and he was one of the best." Mike paused, and the pride gleaming in his eyes told her just how much he still admired his father. "Obviously, with him gone, that business went away, so we've had to come up with something else so we can afford to keep the place. My sister thought of the wedding carriages, and we put a sign on the back to get folks out to the farm and see what all is there."

Lily was fascinated. She'd lived her entire life in cities, and to her one farm was pretty much like another. "What else is there?"

"Last fall, we started up the Oaks Crossing Rescue Center, for injured and abandoned animals. We take in everything from gerbils to draft horses. Yesterday, someone dropped off a beaver with a broken leg, of all things. We figure if people come in and see all the animals for themselves, we can help more wild critters get back into the woods and the pets will have a better chance of finding a home. If you're interested, you can come by sometime. I'd be happy to show you around the farm or the center, whichever you want."

That he was part of such a generous endeavor impressed her enough that she decided her earlier impression of him as being standoffish was due more to her own bad mood the other day than his actual personality. "I'd enjoy seeing both, I'm sure. So many people talk about doing something important, but they never find a way to make it happen."

"Yeah, well, I like animals better than most people I meet, so it works for me."

She clicked her tongue in disapproval. "You don't mean that."

"Actually, I do." His flinty gaze softened a bit, and he almost smiled. "Most of the time, anyway."

She was getting the distinct impression that he was as intrigued by her as she was by him. Whether it was their vastly different backgrounds or their polar-opposite personalities, she couldn't say. But she couldn't deny that the more she learned about him, the more she wanted to know.

And then, out of the blue she heard herself say, "You know, I've always wanted to take riding lessons."

Those icy blue eyes narrowed suspiciously. "Why?"

"Horses are beautiful and strong, and much more intelligent than most people realize."

Giving her a quick once-over, he finished his assessment with a single nod. "True enough."

"I think it would be fun to learn more about them." *And herself,* she added silently. After spending the first twenty-five years of her life being treated as if she'd crumple in the face of any adversity whatsoever, she was eager to test her wings and see how far she could fly. "So what do you think?"

"About teaching you to ride?" She nodded, quelling her impatience while he thought over her proposal. She couldn't understand why he'd turn down a paying customer when his family's business was in such dire straits. Then again, everyone came to decisions in their own way, and she had a feeling that rushing him would end in a curt no-thanks.

"Here's an idea," he offered in a tentative

manner. "I've got some free time this after-noon after four. Why don't we try it once and see how it goes?"

She'd had enough of his boot-dragging, and she let a bit of that anger show in her face. "I'm willing to pay the same rate you charge every-one else. Do you have a problem with teaching me?"

"Not a bit," he replied smoothly. "But you might have a problem learning from me."

"What on earth is *that* supposed to mean?"

Shrugging, he stepped away and turned the doorknob. "I guess we'll find out."

"Fine," she spat, recognizing a challenge when she heard one. "I'll see you at four."

"I'll be in the barn nearest the house. Wear shoes with no heels."

With that, he pulled open the door and strode into the hallway. Her temper was simmering, and she took a few moments to calm down before rejoining her students. As she roamed around the tables offering help and praise as needed, she couldn't get one thing out of her mind.

Like so many of the men she'd known before him, Mike Kinley had severely misjudged her. She was looking forward to showing him just how wrong he was.

* * *

Mike was checking the girth on an English saddle when a yellow convertible drove up and parked near the barns. Lily stepped out of the car, which he couldn't help noticing was nearly as cute as she was. Dressed in jeans and a pink T-shirt, she looked nothing like the well-dressed woman he'd seen up to this point. As a matter of fact, he liked this look much better.

Growling at himself for thinking of her that way, he shook off the impression and took his time strolling over to meet her. The slow pace gave him a chance to remind himself that it was his own fault she was here, and he had no choice but to make the best of it.

Before he got there, Abby came flying down the back porch steps and made a beeline for their visitor.

More excited than usual, she stopped and stared up at her teacher with obvious heroine worship shining in her eyes. "Hi, Miss St. George. Are you ready for your lesson?"

"I think so." She turned to Mike, eyes twinkling in amusement. "I guess we'll find out."

Being a fairly intelligent guy, he recognized that she was punting his own words back at him. Her version was much brighter than his had been, and he got the feeling she was daring him to match her. He managed not to smile, but it wasn't easy in the face of all that perkiness.

Eyeing her sneakers, he frowned. "That's the only pair of flat shoes you own?"

"Obviously," she retorted, tilting her head in a chiding gesture that brought to mind his sassy younger sister.

"Well, you're gonna need some riding boots to grab on to the stirrups. Come on in and I'll see what I've got."

Eager to get her lesson over with, he wasn't crazy about having to go through the extra hoop. It wasn't that he didn't want her in the stable, he told himself as Abby took Lily's hand and tugged her forward. He just wasn't keen about sharing his turf with someone who made him so...jittery.

Inside the sliding door, she fell out of step with him, and he glanced down the rubber aisleway, thinking something must be out of place. The dividing walls between the stalls were made of age-darkened oak, with wrought iron rising from chest height up to the ceiling. Lights and fans dotted the interior, keeping the horses cool on even the hottest days.

It all looked fine to him, and he asked, "Something wrong?"

Eyes wide, she slowly shook her head. "This is incredible. How many spaces are there?"

"Twenty in this barn," he answered proudly, lifting Abby up to sit on a sturdy shelf normally reserved for spare equipment parts. It was currently empty, one more reminder of how close to the bone Dad's beloved Gallimore was operating these days. "The stable for boarders has another fifteen."

"You take care of thirty-five horses here?"

"Well, me and my brothers, Drew and Josh, along with a couple of Dad's old grooms who wanted to stay on after he died."

Peeking into a vacant stall, she looked down the line with obvious disappointment. "They're all outside? I was hoping to meet some of them."

"I saw Gideon waiting in the front paddock for you," Abby piped up helpfully. "First, you need some boots."

"All right, then. Let's find me a pair and get started."

To Mike's ear, the excited pitch of Lily's voice nearly matched his daughter's, and he found himself grinning. In his experience, adults didn't get jazzed about new things the way kids did. Maybe it was being around children all day, he thought, or maybe that was Lily's natural way of viewing the world. Whichever it was, even a reserved guy like him was having a tough time resisting all that enthusiasm.

Stopping outside the tack room, he motioned his prospective student ahead of him. Most folks moved tentatively through the barn during their first visit, but not Lily. She confidently strode past him and into the large storage area. Along one wall were three rows of saddles, some English for dressage and jumping, some Western complete with lassos coiled neatly around their horns. On the other wall, dozens of bridles hung from their padded holders, reins left dangling to avoid straining the leather.

Standing in the middle of it all, Lily spun slowly until she came back to Mike. The look on her face was impossible for him to read, and he waited for her to say something.

"What a great office you have," she commented with a smile. "You must love working here every day."

"Except when it rains. Then it's kinda the pits."

"I guess so," she replied with a laugh. In the corner, something moaned quietly, and she took a hesitant step back. "Did I wake someone up?"

"That's just Sarge," Abby explained. Right on cue, a scruffy blend of several breeds of terrier emerged from the shadows and yawned. "He likes to sleep in here."

Blinking at Lily, the small dog trotted over and sat in front of her, tail wagging politely. Laughing again, she hunkered down and held out her hand for him to sniff. When he was satisfied, he offered a paw that she shook as if he was a small person. "Hello, Sarge. It's a pleasure to meet you."

With a quick yip, he went back toward his spot, glancing over his shoulder in an unspoken request for her to follow him. Which, to Mike's amazement, she did. When she saw the filthy old horse blanket he had there, she turned to Mike with a curious expression. "Is that really where he sleeps?"

"I know it looks bad, but he likes it that way."

"Why?"

"It's kind of a long story."

"That's okay," she said, sitting down on the scuffed plank floor to pet the dog. "I like stories."

Mike had planned on getting through her lesson as quickly and painlessly as possible. Since he didn't want to seem rude, he put aside his impatience and carefully balanced himself on a three-legged stool. "Well, his owner was an older lady who lived in the area. She had a horse named Captain that she'd owned since he was a foal, and he was getting on in years himself. When his stablemate died, she was afraid he'd be lonely, so she got him a dog."

"Sarge." Lily smiled down at the mutt, who seemed to be listening intently to his story. "What a nice thing for her to do."

"Last year, she got really sick and had to move into a nursing home. She asked me to take the two of them and make sure they stayed together. One of Captain's blankets dropped off the side of the stall one day, and Sarge took to sleeping on it while he kept his friend company. Now Captain's gone, and this little guy refuses to sleep anywhere else."

"That is so touching," she murmured in a voice filled with sympathy. Smiling down at the dog, she cooed, "If we all had such faithful friends who'd stick by us no matter what, our lives would be so much better."

Even though she wasn't speaking to him, Mike caught the wistfulness in her tone. At some point, someone had disappointed this bright, engaging woman. While it had absolutely nothing to do with him, just the thought of it made him angry.

"What's this?" she asked, fingering a label sewn to the corner of the blanket. Giving Mike a knowing grin, she said, "It says 'do not wash.'"

"My sister Erin's a neat freak, and she's in

charge of keeping the blankets and saddle pads clean. That one—" he pointed "—still smells like his old buddy, and Sarge likes it that way. I figure one dirty blanket more or less doesn't make much difference."

"Not to you maybe," Lily told him with an admiring smile, "but to him it means a lot. It's so considerate of you to recognize that. That must be why his owner chose you to take care of her animals. She trusted you to do what was best for them."

Mike wasn't accustomed to being praised for simply following his instincts, and he shifted uncomfortably in his seat. "Most folks'd probably think it's nuts."

"I think it's sweet," she corrected him in a gentle but firm voice that he imagined worked wonders on her students.

Hoping to joke his way out of an awkward situation, he forced a chuckle. "I'd appreciate you not spreading that around."

"Deal."

Standing, she brushed her hands off on her jeans and looked over the beat-up collection of riding boots that had found their way onto the shelves. Some had been outgrown, others donated. One pair had even been tossed at Mike's head whcn a young diva-in-training threw a world-class tantrum and stormed out of her one and only lesson. When he shared that detail with Lily, she laughed again. This woman did that more than anyone he knew, and he had to admit the light, carefree sound was beginning to grow on him.

"Well, you don't have to worry about that kind of nonsense with me," she assured him. "If I end up being a hopelessly terrible rider, I'll assume it's my fault, not yours."

She reached toward the upper shelf where the smallest sizes were, but she couldn't quite stretch far enough.

"Here, let me." To his surprise, she pointed out a pair of well-worn brown boots that had once belonged to his mother. "You sure? They're kinda plain."

"They look like they've had a lot of experience. Maybe they'll help me catch on quicker."

Interesting theory, he mused as he brought them down for her. Sitting on a chair outside the storage room, she shed her sneakers and pulled on the boots. They seemed to work, and she held out her feet to admire them. Then, to his surprise, she looked up at the shelf where Abby was perched. "What do you think of these?"

"Perfect," she announced, her ponytail bobbing as she nodded. "Just like Cinderella."

"Well, don't get your hopes up," he teased. "We're fresh out of princes around here."

For some reason, Lily's smile disintegrated, and she sighed. "I've had my fill of princes. The ones I meet always seem to turn into frogs."

Mike wasn't sure what to say to that, so he decided it was best to ignore the comment. "Ready for your lesson?"

"Definitely." She shook off her momentary funk, and that playful grin was back. "Are you?"

Despite his plan to keep a professional distance from her, he found himself returning her smile. "I guess we'll find out."

He strolled over and let Abby climb onto his shoulders, then lowered her to the floor.

"Daddy, can I go have a snack with Grammy while you give Lily her lesson?"

"Sure, but save me some of those cookies. They smell real good."

She thanked him with a quick hug, and he smiled as he watched her zoom back toward the house. Hard as it had been for him to leave his ranch foreman's job in New Mexico behind, his daughter was happy here, surrounded by his large, chaotic family and now a class full of new friends. Much as he hated losing his independence, her happiness made it all worth it to him.

Hauling his mind back to reality, he led the way through a sliding door that opened onto the paddock where Gideon was dozing in the sun. When Lily moved out of his sight, Sarge let out a pitiful whimper and jumped up to follow her. To Mike's knowledge, the dog had never shown much affection for anyone but Captain. That he seemed to have taken a shine to the soft-spoken teacher had to mean something. But right now, Mike couldn't for the life of him figure out what it was.

Chapter Three

"Seriously?" Swiveling toward Mike, she gave him a horrified look. "You couldn't find a slightly smaller horse for me?"

"Give him a chance," the trainer cajoled, rubbing the enormous animal's chest as if he was a golden retriever. "Gideon's the gentlest horse on the farm. Abby rides him all the time."

Clearly, that last comment was meant to goad her into leaping onto the saddle that looked to be five precarious feet above the ground. Shaking her head, Lily announced, "She's a lot braver than I am."

"I doubt that. Most folks'd be terrified to take on a roomful of kindergarteners all on their own for the first time, but you did just fine with them. After that, this guy should be a piece of cake."

"You thought I did well today?" she blurted without thinking how it might sound to him. It was a good thing she wasn't trying to impress this man, she thought ruefully. Coming across as needy was bad enough, but add in a heavy dose of insecurity and most men understandably ran for the hills.

"You were great with them," he said without hesitation. "Kids are like animals—they know a phony when they see one, and from where I was sitting, I could tell they really liked you."

His praise rang with sincerity, and she smiled. "That's nice of you to say."

"Like I told you the other day, I don't say things just to be nice. The truth's not always easy to hear, but at least it doesn't change from one day to the next."

Someone had lied to this man, she realized with sudden clarity. Someone he trusted enough to care very much that the person had deceived him. Since she already suspected that this devoted single father was divorced, it didn't take a rocket scientist to guess that someone had been his ex-wife. Lily was definitely curious about what had happened to their marriage, but she'd never dream of asking a virtual stranger such an intensely—and probably hurtful—personal question.

Instead, she refocused her attention on the

horse standing quietly in the middle of the fenced-in space. Now that she'd calmed down a bit, she registered the fact that he was more than big. He was powerfully built and covered in scruffy brown fur that made her think of a retro-style shag rug. To add to his unusual appearance, there was an off-kilter white star on his forehead that led to a strip of white that zigzagged down along the right side of his nose.

As they stared at each other, his large brown eyes shone with intelligence, and she was almost certain he was taking stock of her the same way she was doing with him. The corner of his mouth crinkled, and she couldn't help laughing. "Is he smiling at me?"

"I'd imagine so. He really likes people."

Puzzled by Mike's tone, she glanced at him. "You sound surprised by that."

"If you knew what this old boy's been through—" Mike fondly ruffled the horse's shaggy mane "—you'd be surprised, too."

That did it for her. Sympathy for the rescued animal flooded Lily's heart, and she put aside her earlier reluctance to approach him. He nuzzled her hand, and on her other side, she felt something tap her arm. Looking down, she realized Mike had a few apple slices and was trying to sneak them to her.

"Hold your palm out flat." He demonstrated

for her. "He's pretty careful, but if you curl your fingers he might nip you by mistake."

"Okay." Still a little nervous, she held the apples out for Gideon, who blew on her hand before delicately taking a piece from her. His lips tickled her skin, making her giggle like one of her students.

When she was out of treats, he slurped her hand in an equine thank-you and just about knocked her over when he started rubbing his forehead on her shoulder. Thankfully, Mike steadied her until she could brace herself more firmly. "He's really strong."

"He's a Belgian draft horse. Most of him, anyway." Scratching him between the eyes, Mike continued. "The rest, I'm not so sure about, but it doesn't matter much. He's got a great heart, and that's good enough for me."

Now that she'd seen him in his natural element, Lily was beginning to notice a pattern in the gruff trainer's personality. He wasn't crazy about humans, but he was wonderful with animals. Considering all the troubles she'd been having lately, she had to admit he might have the right idea, after all. "He seems to like you, too."

"Yeah, well, he's pretty easy to impress."

"Easier than people?"

Mike's eyes narrowed with sudden displeasure. "You sound like my ex-wife."

"I'm sorry," she stammered, feeling awful for inadvertently hitting what was obviously a sore point. "I didn't mean to stir up bad memories."

They stared at each other for a few self-conscious moments, and then he shrugged. "It's no big deal. We fought all the time, so the divorce was actually a relief."

She recognized his response as brave words meant to conceal the pain darkening his features. He made her think of a child who'd had his feelings hurt but stubbornly refused to own up to it. Hoping to lift his spirits, she said, "Maybe she just didn't understand you very well. With some people, you have to work a little harder, but in the end they're worth the effort."

"Aw, man," he groaned, "you really are an optimist, aren't you?"

It sounded as if he was accusing her of some kind of crime, and Lily's reflex was to bristle the way she had the first time they met. Then it struck her that this was an opportunity to bend his opinion of her in a more positive direction.

Giving him her sweetest smile, she said, "It works for me."

To her amazement, his frown mellowed into

a crooked half grin. "Can't argue with that. So whattya say? Are you ready to give ol' Gideon a whirl?"

He punctuated his invitation with a black velvet hard hat, and she knew this was the moment of truth. Either she was going to go through with this, or she'd leave Gallimore Stables in disgrace. Because she was a St. George, she chose the first one. "Absolutely."

Taking the helmet from him, she fastened it on and moved to stand beside the horse. Mike gave her a boost into the saddle and helped her get her feet settled in the stirrups.

"Okay up there?" he asked.

"More or less." Her heart was already moving at a fast trot, and all she'd done so far was get on. Mike seemed to sense that, because he had her lean forward and back in the saddle, then bend from one side to the other. Once he'd convinced her that she was fairly safe, things got more interesting.

Her teacher strolled to the center of the ring and stood with his hands in the front pockets of his jeans as if he didn't have a care in the world. "Take him out on the rail and let him walk."

"I'm not taking him anywhere," Lily replied in a voice that shook a lot more than she'd have preferred. "He's in charge."

"Just 'cause he's bigger than you doesn't mean he's in charge," Mike corrected her in a patient voice that told her he'd said those exact same words many times. "He might be stronger, but you're smarter. The trick is to make him think it's his idea."

How on earth was she supposed to do that? Lily wondered. Then she recalled Mike's comment about animals being similar to kids, and she decided it couldn't hurt to try treating Gideon like one of her students. "All right, big guy. Let's try walking along the rail."

Nothing. The horse patiently stood there, apparently content to watch his stablemates munching away out in the pasture. When she heard a low chuckle, she glared over at her not-so-amusing instructor. "Are you making fun of me?"

"Guess I wasn't very clear. Give him a nudge with your heels and bring your reins to the left."

She noticed he didn't deny he'd been laughing at her, but since her life was pretty much in his hands, she decided now wasn't the time to take issue with his prickly personality. She followed his suggestion, and to her astonishment, the Belgian obeyed her instantly, plodding over to the track that had been worn in the ground.

As they circled the small space, she was awestruck by the power she felt rippling underneath her. This brawny animal could crush her without any effort at all, but here they were, moving in the same direction together. Slowly, to be sure, but it was a huge accomplishment for someone who'd lived her entire life being treated like a rare flower in a greenhouse.

"You're looking good, Lily. How does it feel?"

"Incredible." Gaining confidence, she reached down to pat Gideon's flexing neck. "You're such a good boy."

The Belgian blew a raspberry and seemed to nod in agreement, making her laugh. They did a few circuits each way, even trotting for a while to keep things from getting boring. The rest of her promised half hour passed by in a flash, and she had a hard time remembering why she'd been so nervous at the beginning.

In what was apparently his customary way of handling any situation, without preamble Mike came forward and took the reins from her. "I think that was a good first lesson. Why don't we quit while we're ahead?"

"That's fine. It's pretty hot, and we don't want to overtax him."

Her comment sparked something in those icy blue eyes, and they warmed just a touch when they settled on her. Then it was gone, and she wondered if she'd imagined the whole thing. He helped her down, then removed the horse's tack so deftly, she wouldn't be the least bit shocked to learn he could manage the task blindfolded.

He balanced everything on the top rail and opened a gate that led out to the front pasture. "All set, boy."

Clearly delighted, the gelding shook himself out, then loped through the opening to join his buddies at the far end. Lily admired them for a few moments, savoring the peaceful end to a hectic day. Between moving into the room she'd rented in town and prepping for school, she hadn't had any free time since her sister's wedding. It felt good to stand here in the sunshine and breathe in the warm, hay-scented air.

But she knew Mike had things to do, so she dragged her eyes away from the beautiful scene and smiled up at him. "So, did I pass muster?"

"Sorry?"

"Are you willing to take me on as one of your students, or do you need more time to decide?"

"Oh, that." Shaking his head, he chuckled as they started walking toward her car. "I guess we can make it work. What day's good for you?"

"How about Fridays at four? It would make a great start to my weekends."

"So you're staying in town after school's done, then?"

"My lease goes through the end of August. After that—"

She shrugged, and for some odd reason he frowned. "You don't have a job for the fall?"

"I've been told something might open up at the elementary school, but right now there's nothing available. We'll see what happens."

Just as they reached the driveway, she heard a familiar voice chirping her name, and she turned to find Abby running over to join them. "I'm so glad you're still here! Grammy said to bring you in to meet her. Y'know, since you're my new teacher and all."

"Miss St. George is a busy lady, Abs. We don't wanna hold her up."

"Oh, I have time." Smiling down at her student, she added, "Abby's told me a lot about your mother, and I'd love to meet her."

"I can just imagine what you've been hearing from our little one," a woman's voice chimed in from the front porch. The accent had a musical lilt to it that reminded Lily of her late great-grandmother Katie, who'd stepped off a boat from Ireland and into a career that took her from the garment factories of New York to the homes of high-society women up and down the East Coast. It was in one of them that she'd met the dashing Alexander St. George, and the rest was history.

That image sparked wonderful memories for Lily, and she faced the woman with a smile. "It's a pleasure to meet you, Mrs. Kinley."

"None of that now," she protested, waving off the formality with a hand dusted with flour. "It's Maggie to everyone hereabouts. Including you."

"Thank you. And I'm Lily."

"That you are." Flashing a dimpled smile, she turned to her son with a disapproving look. "Michael, aren't you going to invite this lovely young lady inside for something to drink on this hot day?"

"I think you just did that." He scowled back, but the fondness twinkling in his eyes betrayed him. So, he wasn't such a grumbly bear, after all, Lily noted. It made a girl wonder what else was going on behind that lopsided grin.

"Come on," Abby urged, grasping Lily's hand to pull her up the steps. "We've been making chocolate chip cookies. They're still all gooey, so we have to eat them fast."

"My favorite kind. It smells like you put extra chocolate in them, too."

"That's how Daddy likes them." Flashing him an adoring look, she grinned. "Isn't it, Daddy?"

"Got that right."

He returned her look with an ease that astonished Lily. Up until now, she'd viewed him as a tightly reined-in kind of guy who wasn't exactly the mushy type. But when he looked at his daughter, she saw a side of him she'd have never in a million years guessed he had. The more she got to know the gruff horse trainer, the more she liked him. That wasn't the best idea for her, she cautioned herself. Getting involved with the father of one of her students— no matter how fascinating he might be—was definitely not going to happen. She had no intention of jeopardizing her teaching career by starting out with such a foolish mistake.

So, since anything serious with him was off the table, she resolved to keep him at a polite, professional distance. *It shouldn't be too hard,* she reasoned. He was clearly doing the same with her, although she didn't quite understand why. Normally, she had to push men away when she discovered they were more interested in making nice with her well-connected family than in dating her. Because of her evasive maneuvers during their first meeting, Mike had no idea who she was, but for some reason he was still keeping his distance. While that suited her in one sense, in another it made her want to find out why.

That wasn't likely to happen today, so she took a seat next to Abby on a bench at the large oak table in the Kinleys' kitchen. The sprawling white farmhouse had a comfortable feel to it, from the bright windows letting in sunlight and a soft breeze, to the mellowed wood of the carved cabinets that lined the walls. "Maggie, you have a beautiful home. How old is it?"

"Nearly a hundred years," she answered as she piled cookies onto a plate. "My husband, Justin—God rest him—inherited the place from his granddad who moved here from Ireland just before the First World War. Back then, they trained horses for the military, then Justin and his father got into the racing business. And our boys, of course."

"I just broke 'em in," Mike clarified. "Dad made 'em into winners."

The pride in his voice was tinged with sorrow, and Lily said, "He sounds like a wonderful man. I'm so sorry you lost him."

"You have to make time to dance every single day," Maggie advised as she set the cookies on the table and sat down beside her son.

"You never know how many songs the Good Lord will grant you."

"Is that an old Irish blessing?" Lily asked.

"Justin's," Maggie replied with a nostalgic smile. "No matter how tired he was at the end of a day, he always took me for a spin."

"You've got the broken toes to prove it," Mike teased, and she laughed.

"That's the truth of it. I adored that man, but he wasn't light of foot, to be sure."

"Grampa used to dance with me, too," Abby said, pointing to a collection of family photos on the wall. One was of a large man wearing suspenders and a flannel shirt who bore a strong resemblance to Mike. Gazing down at the tiny bundle he held cradled in his muscular arms, the man had a delighted smile that reminded her of the way Mike had looked at his daughter earlier. Lily was touched by the way the strong Kinley men seemed to melt in Abby's presence.

Despite his brusque demeanor, she could easily see that Mike had inherited more than his father's build and good looks. Recognizing that, she felt her vow to keep him at arm's length beginning to waver. Maybe these riding lessons weren't the best idea she'd ever had. If she was smart, she'd invent a reason to stop coming to the farm and avoid the temptation of getting closer to Mike. If only she didn't feel so at home here, she added with a mental sigh. The animals were enticing enough, but now that she'd met more of his family, she liked the place even more.

"So," Maggie said while she handed Lily an icy glass of sweet tea, "how was your first lesson on Gideon?"

"I'm not ready for an equestrian team yet, but I think it went pretty well."

"I'm afraid I'm not much of a teacher," Mike confessed with a grimace. "Gideon did his best, though."

This was her chance to begin creating that space she'd just been pondering, but she couldn't bring herself to let the poor man believe he'd failed her somehow. "You both did, and I really appreciate it."

That got her a grateful look, as if he wasn't accustomed to being praised for what he did. Something about this man tugged at her soft heart, and any thoughts of ending her lessons disappeared. After all, it wasn't as if she'd be dating him, so that wouldn't cross the professional line she'd drawn. And as her social-butterfly mother had often told her, you could never have too many friends. Recalling that upbeat advice, she smiled and made a mental note to call Mom later for a chat. An unapologetic free spirit, she'd been divorced from Lily's father longer than they'd been married and spent most of her time exploring one fascinating place or another. She was in Barcelona these days, and it had been two weeks since their last call—way too long.

Abby finished chewing her cookie, then looked at Mike with shining eyes. "Daddy, I just had a mindstorm."

"Brainstorm," he corrected her with a chuckle. "What is it?"

"At lunch today, I was telling my friends how when we lived on the ranch, you taught me how to ride when I was three. They thought it was really cool, and some of them wished they could learn, too."

"Yeah? Which ones?"

"Kennedy, Brianna, Jillian." She added several more names, ticking them off until she ran out of fingers. Then she cocked her head with a chiding look. "They're all real. Ask Miss St. George."

Obviously smothering a grin, Mike flashed Lily a somber look. Having gotten used to spending most of her time in her own company, she was pleased to be included in the Kinleys' lighthearted banter. Playing her role, she held up her hand. "Scout's honor."

His gaze refocused on his daughter. "And you're saying they want me to teach them?"

"Everyone thought you were really cool when you came in for show-and-tell. Especially Peter."

"The boy whose dad died last year?" She nodded, and some of the skepticism left his eyes. Lily understood that he felt a kinship with the fatherless boy, and her estimation of the reserved horse trainer rose a few more notches.

Maggie tsked in sympathy. "I remember hearing about that. Such a tragedy for those children to lose their father so young. I'm sure we can find a way to do something for Peter, at least."

"Well, we can't tell him yes and the others no," Mike pointed out in a resigned tone. Sending Lily a "help me" look, he went on. "If we offer him lessons, we have to do the same for everyone in Abby's class."

She'd love to give him an out, since he was making no secret of the fact that he wasn't totally thrilled with the idea. But Lily knew how much it would mean to several of the children, not to mention Abby. Playing host to her friends at the farm would turn her into a minor celebrity, and despite his standoffish demeanor Lily suspected Mike might actually enjoy it.

"That's the best approach with kids. That way no one feels left out."

"You should come, too, Miss St. George," Abby breathed excitedly. "You could keep us all quiet and in line, just like you do when we're at school. And Daddy can work with the horses, 'cause he's good at that."

While Maggie didn't say a word, her hazel eyes glimmered with her opinion. Abby's glowed like a clear sky, but Mike's were a murky blend of blue and gray. The color had more than a tinge of warning to it, and Lily was inclined to take it seriously.

"I don't know, honey. That's a pretty big commitment for your father and me to make when we're already busy with other things." By Abby's puzzled expression, Lily assumed she'd used a word beyond the girl's six-year-old vocabulary. "What I mean is, we wouldn't want to get started and then have to disappoint you and your friends because it takes too much time."

"You could just do a few lessons," she argued, her eyes beginning to well. "I'll help, I promise."

"I don't mean to sound greedy," Maggie said, "but the money would come in handy around here. If enough children sign up, maybe you could even take a few less wedding jobs," she added, giving her son a prodding look.

A glint of humor warmed his eyes, and he shook his head with a good-natured grin. "You sure know how to hit a guy where he lives. Why don't you two schemers wait in here while I talk to Miss St. George outside?"

Lily appreciated him giving her the chance to flee if she chose not to sign on, so she excused herself and followed him to the door. The screen creaked as he opened it and held it open for her to go out ahead of him. When they reached the far end of the rambling porch, he leaned back against the railing and folded his arms with a sigh. "Sorry about that. I had no clue that was coming."

"A Kinley tag team," she commented with a light laugh. "They're good."

"Tell me about it." After a moment, he went on. "Look, if you're not into this, it's really no big deal. Riding herd on a bunch of rug rats isn't my first choice of things to do, so if it never happens, I'd be okay with that."

Something in his voice tipped her off, and she tilted her head with a smile. "You're a terrible liar. The minute Abby started tearing up, you decided to go along and give her friends riding lessons."

"Yeah," he grumbled, staring up at the beadboard ceiling of the porch roof. Coming back to Lily, he went on in a wry tone. "When they handed her to me at the hospital, I knew there'd never be anything I wouldn't do for her. Sappy, huh?"

"Sweet," Lily corrected him quickly. "I guess that makes her Daddy's girl."

"You must know something about that yourself."

"I used to." The words slipped out before she could stop them, and Lily cringed at the slicing bitterness she heard. Attempting to blunt the edge, she continued. "Dad and I don't see eye to eye on too many things these days. You must know what I mean. I'm sure your father wasn't too excited about you leaving the family business to strike out on your own."

"Actually, he was. We worked well together, but he always knew I'd have to make my own way eventually. After Abby was born, he and Mom came out to visit us at the ranch I managed in New Mexico." Pausing, he gave her a sad smile. "He said he admired me for being my own man and making a good life for my family. I was never prouder in my life."

"That's wonderful. Good for him."

Lily couldn't help envying Mike's solid relationship with his father. With the St. Georges, sons went into the family business, and daughters were expected to marry someone of the proper standing to join the fold. Natalie had lived up to her obligation, but Lily simply couldn't bring herself to stick with the plan. Everyone but her generous grandfather considered her one step shy of a straitjacket, but she was pretty sure her plucky great-grandma Katie was up in heaven cheering her on.

"Doing your own thing isn't easy," Mike said, "but I can promise you it's worth it."

He gave her a sympathetic look that told her he'd picked up on things she hadn't meant to tell him. She wasn't sure what to make of his perceptiveness, but in that brief moment, she got a glimpse of what Abby must see in him. A serious man with a dry sense of humor who loved her with everything he had and would find a way to give her the moon if she asked him for it. That's how he must have been with his wife, Lily knew instinctively. And again, she couldn't help wondering what had gone wrong between them.

"What?" he asked.

"Nothing."

"This ain't my first rodeo, sweetheart," he informed her with the scowl he so frequently used. "That look you're wearing means trouble with a capital *T*."

"It's none of my business."

"That never stops any woman in this family." His tone was less cynical now, but only slightly. He gave her a "go ahead" look, and she decided this was as good a time as any to satisfy her curiosity about his divorce once and for all.

"I'm just wondering about you and your ex," she began awkwardly. When he didn't respond, she took it as a prompt for her to continue. "You mentioned her earlier, but you didn't say much. Was it a friendly split?"

"It was pretty one-sided. Dana left us when Abby was a year old, and beyond getting her signature on the divorce papers, we haven't heard from her since."

Delivered in a monotone, those words were devoid of emotion, but there was plenty of it crackling in his eyes. Bitterness and disgust battled for space, and the harsh set of his jaw told her precisely how much that betrayal still angered him. Lily had never met the woman, but she was human enough to acknowledge that she pretty much hated Dana, too. "That's awful. My parents are divorced, but they both always made sure I knew how much they loved me. How could Dana abandon her family like that?"

"If it was just me, I could've taken it," he explained in a low voice seething with rage. "We had our problems, but that was no reason for her to walk out on her own child the way she did. I'm just glad Abby doesn't remember any of it. I don't know how I'd explain it to her."

Lily was beginning to see how his mind worked, and she had to admit she was impressed. His anger wasn't for himself, but for the daughter he cherished. Lily had run up against more egotistical men throughout her life than she cared to recall. Finding one who put others before himself was a refreshing change.

Putting that very personal observation aside, she got back to why they'd come out here in the first place. "So, about me helping with the riding school."

He shrugged. "Totally up to you. I'm good with a partner or going solo."

His intent to do the lessons with or without her help belied his casual indifference. Something told her that he was the kind of guy who feigned carelessness to avoid giving people too close a look at his heart. Which, judging by his gentle treatment of animals and children, was a lot bigger than he probably cared to admit.

"Well, let's try it for a while," she finally decided. "I can at lcast gct you started until you and the kids are better acquainted with each other. After a couple weeks, you might be fine on your own."

"Or hopelessly insane. Could go either way."

Laughing, they shook hands to seal their arrangement.

"Y'know, you're gonna make my daughter's day."

"Should we go tell her the good news?" Lily asked with a smile. She'd tensed up at one point while they were talking, and he got the feeling their conversation had plucked a nerve for her. He hardly knew her, but he hated to think he'd done something—even inadvertently—to upset this sweet-natured woman.

"After you."

The second they were back in the kitchen, Abby's face lit up as if it was Christmas morning. "We can really do lessons?"

"Sure," he agreed with a mock growl. "What else've I got to do all summer?"

"Thank you, Daddy!" Launching herself at him, she wrapped her arms around his waist in the kind of hug he'd never get enough of if he lived a hundred years. Then, to his surprise, she reached out one hand and pulled Lily in, too. Beaming up at her new friend, she said, "And thank you, Miss St. George. Having you here will make things so much better."

Lily tilted her head in obvious confusion. "For who?"

"All of us," Abby announced confidently. "And I promise to help with everything. I'll tell all my friends, and we'll make tons of money to keep the farm running. Right, Grammy?"

She glanced over at the woman still seated at the table, hands folded in front of her in a pose Mike knew all too well. She'd been praying, and he fought the scowl threatening to break through. She knew exactly how he felt about all that religious nonsense, but she'd gone over his head and directly to God, who'd made it clear that He'd lost interest in Mike long ago.

"I was thinking," Lily began as she and Abby sat side by side on the bench, "we could design a logo for our school. Then we can print up flyers and maybe get some T-shirts made for the students. They'd enjoy having them, and when they wear them around town, other people will notice and get interested in taking lessons, too. If we get enough students, we could even have a horse show at the end of the summer. That would bring lots of people to the farm to see the great work you're all doing with the animals here."

Mike wasn't sure how they'd gone from a few lessons to a full-blown circus, but he had to admit her idea had merit. Not only would it give the students something to work toward, when their families attended the show Gallimore Stables would get the kind of exposure it needed so desperately. He'd been racking his brain for months for a killer idea, and Lily had come up with a winner in the space of a single conversation. Amazing.

"That's a great suggestion," he commented with none of his usual reservations. "It could be just the thing we need to help us get back on track."

"I'm glad you think so." Giving him a grateful smile, she focused back on Abby. "Do you have any ideas for our logo?"

"Sure!" Popping up from her seat, Abby fetched a stack of blank paper and her tub of crayons from the rolltop desk in the corner. One of the many antiques his mother had lovingly collected and restored, over the years it had been everything from the farm's bookkeeping space to storage for an endless jumble of paperwork. Now it was Abby's art center, with her latest projects proudly displayed on the corkboard behind it.

"I don't think Lily meant now," Mike cautioned his energetic girl as gently as he could.

"No time like the present," Lily corrected him with the kind of chipper tone that would have come across as forced from anyone else.

With her curly ponytail and sparkling blue eyes, though, it suited her perfectly.

Uh-oh, he thought glumly. That was no way for him to be thinking about his daughter's teacher. And new business partner. When that realization struck him, he sat down and gazed across the table at Lily. "Before we get all caught up in this, I think we should discuss the setup for this school."

"What do you mean?" she asked, fingertipping through the crayon box until she found the right shade of green for the grass she was sketching.

"We'll be making money from the lessons," he explained, not sure why it was even necessary. To him, the reason for laying everything out on the table was a common-sense leap anyone should have been able to make on their own. "You'll be doing half the work, so you should get half the profits."

Without any delay to think it over, she said, "Tell you what. I'll take twenty-five percent and free lessons for myself."

"You're kidding, right?"

Lifting her eyes from her drawing, she shook her head. "Totally serious."

"You're not much of a businesswoman, are you?" he asked with a chuckle.

"Not a bit." She gave him a sweet smile that had an unsettling edge to it. "Is that a problem?"

"Not for me, but you might change your mind later on."

"I know what I'm doing, Mike," she assured him in that musical drawl he'd admired the first time they met. "It's not easy being in a new place and not knowing anyone. It might sound corny, but spending some of my summer here on this beautiful farm will be a dream come true for me."

Stunned by the revelation, he stared over at the slender young woman who'd dropped into his life in the strangest way he could possibly imagine. Sincerity shone in her eyes, and he felt something rustling inside him, as if it had been asleep for a long time and was starting to wake up again.

Doing his best to ignore that, he tried to look cool. "Okay, then. Works for me."

"This is supposed to be Gideon," Abby said, angling the picture for their guest to see. "I can't get his head right, Miss St. George. Could you help me?"

"Absolutely." Lily took the page and adjusted the lines into a stylized horse's silhouette. "When it's just us, you can call me Lily. As long as that's okay with your father and your grandma."

"Wonderful idea," Maggie approved, nodding as she got to her feet. "I've got laundry to tend to, but when I come back, I'm curious to see what sort of ideas you three come up with."

Mike knew that tone, and it had nothing to do with the usual "work first" advice she'd doled out to him and his siblings all their lives. He was as far from an artist as you could get and would be little to no help with designing a logo for the riding school. Which she knew perfectly well. That could mean only one thing, and he wasn't thrilled about her pathetically transparent attempt to throw Lily and him together.

Cocking his head, he gave his romantic mother a warning glare. Which she didn't see because she was already walking away from the table.

Chapter Four

It was a good thing for him that Lily was here.

Mike had only three riding students on the first day, but they were a real handful. Kennedy was so wired, he kept waiting for her to burst from all the excitement. Brianna kept nibbling the apple slices she was supposed to save for Sparkle, the dappled gray pony who was patiently enduring all their attention.

And then there was Peter. With a nest of dark hair and huge brown eyes, by turns he looked thrilled to be here and scared to death. Mike had a knack for reading horses to gauge what they needed from him, but other people's kids, not so much. Lily, on the other hand, was an expert.

"Peter," she called out softly, "Sparkle's mane is pretty tangled on this side. Why don't you come help me straighten it out?"

There was absolutely nothing wrong with the mare's grooming, and Mike came close to telling her so. Then he realized that she was trying to make their student feel more comfortable around the pony and decided it was best to keep his mouth shut. After some hemming and hawing, Peter edged cautiously around the horse and watched while Lily combed her fingers through the long, silky strands. The boy copied her motion, and Mike looked on in amazement as his semiterrified expression gave way to a tentative smile.

"She's really pretty," he said, lightly patting her neck.

"Girls like hearing that," Lily commented, flashing a playful grin up at Mike. "Don't they, Mr. Kinley?"

There was no resisting that look, so he didn't even bother trying. Instead, he met the challenge and smiled back. "So I've heard."

"Can any of you tell me what a girl horse is called?" Lily asked, hunkering down to put her on a level with the kids clustered around her. They all raised their hands as if they were still in her classroom, and Mike swallowed a chuckle to avoid embarrassing anyone. "Kennedy?"

"A mare," the perky redhead answered confidently. "A boy horse is a stallion."

"That's right," Lily commented, wiping her hands on her jeans as she stood. "Sparkle looks like she's ready for a rider now. Who wants to go first?"

Crickets.

Mike bit back a groan, wondering why their overly optimistic parents had signed them up for riding lessons if they were scared of a horse whose dainty ears barely reached his shoulders. Abby was fearless by nature, and spending her life around animals of all sizes had made her so bold, he wasn't prepared for her friends to be the exact opposite.

Fortunately, she was just outside the fence, keeping silent as a mouse the way she'd promised before they started. When he raised his eyebrows at her, she took his cue and clambered over the rail with the practiced motion of a rodeo star.

"Here, guys," she offered brightly. "Watch me."

Plunking a helmet over her braids, she swung into the saddle as if she'd been born there and nudged Sparkle into a walk and then a mellow trot. Guiding the pony with a sure hand, she circled the ring and did a figure eight in the middle, just the way he'd taught her. In spite of her age, she handled it all with the grace of a self-assured teenager, and Mike knew he'd just been granted a glimpse of what was coming down the road for them both.

Part of him felt proud to know he was part of the reason she was growing into such a fine young lady. Another part—the one that made him crazy sometimes—dreaded the day she met up with a young man who recognized how incredible she was. Since no father ever born could stop the inevitable, Mike pushed the worry back into its dark corner and let himself enjoy the moment.

Halting in the center and facing her friends, Abby dropped the reins and held out her hands. "See? It's easy, and way more fun than watching."

Her little demonstration was just the trick, and their three guests lined up behind Lily, clamoring for a turn. After cautioning them to stay calm and quiet, she helped Kennedy into the seat and pointed over to the rail. "Just copy what Abby showed you, and you'll be fine. Sparkle knows what to do."

While Mike had great confidence in the pony's gentle demeanor, he figured it was best to stay alert as he edged farther into the small area. He'd put the softest rubber bit he had in the bridle, which was a good thing because this girl was sawing on the reins as if she was trying to start a fire.

"Just hold them still down on her neck," he advised in what he hoped came across as a helpful tone. "She knows where you want her to go."

"How?"

"Horses are pretty smart." *Smarter than most people,* he nearly added before thinking better of it. He was being paid to teach children to ride horses, he reminded himself, not destroy their innocent view of the world in general.

When he judged that they'd gone on long enough, he spiraled his finger in the air in the "wrap it up" signal he and Lily had arranged earlier. Nodding, she stepped in to take Sparkle's reins and help Kennedy down before boosting Brittany on. Her session went pretty much the same way, and then it was Peter's turn.

Mike couldn't deny he had a special interest in this particular student. They had something very sober in common, and hard as it had been for him to absorb the grief of losing his father, he couldn't imagine how tough it was for a child. He wanted to do something for this little guy, to let him know someone understood how he was feeling.

Since he didn't have Lily's gentle touch, Mike recognized that sharing his training expertise was the best he could do. He only hoped it would help somehow.

The boy seemed more self-assured around the horse now, and he listened intently to both Lily's and Mike's instructions. When a squawking blue jay landed on the fence post near her head, Sparkle abruptly lurched to the side and started prancing away from it.

"There, there," Peter crooned, patting her neck in a soothing gesture. "It's just a noisy little bird. You're okay."

He didn't yank on the reins or grab the saddle horn in a death grip the way most adults would have done. Instead, he let the mare have her head and waited for her to settle. When she did, he smiled and ruffled her mane. "There's a good girl, Sparkle. You're doing fine."

"That was fantastic, Peter," Mike praised him without hesitation, strolling over to meet them. "You calmed her down in record time. I'm real impressed."

"I didn't want her to be scared." Staring down at the reins clutched in his pudgy fingers, he added, "It's no fun to be scared."

Resting a hand on his shoulder, Mike waited for the boy to meet his eyes. "No, it's not. It takes a brave person to make someone else feel safe."

"I'm not brave. I'm just a kid."

"From what I've seen, you've got more courage than most grown-ups do their whole lives."

Peter's miserable expression morphed into joy, and his eyes suddenly glowed with pride. "Thanks, Mr. Kinley."

"Anytime. Since you're the last one on, how'd you like to walk Sparkle back to the stable for a rubdown?"

"Awesome!" Seeming to catch himself, he took a breath and more quietly said, "Yes, please."

Chuckling, Mike rumpled his unruly hair and strode on ahead of him. It was almost dinnertime, and Sparkle followed sedately in his tracks, sniffing at his pockets for the oat treats he always kept there.

In the barn, Mike supervised while the kids untacked their equine friend and showered her with compliments and hugs while they brushed her coat. She ate up all the attention, and Mike was fairly certain that if she'd been human, her head would've ended up being twice its usual size by the time they were done.

They turned her out into the pasture with her stablemates and walked over to the house, where three cars were parked in the turnaround. After assuring the children's parents that everything had gone according to plan, Mike was surprised to discover he wasn't as glad to have the first lesson over with as he'd anticipated.

"Huh," he grunted to no one in particular. Since he didn't say anything beyond that, he was surprised when Lily laughed.

"Not as bad as you were expecting?"

"Not even close. 'Course, I had some help." Catching Abby in a one-armed hug, he grinned down at her. "You were a real trouper out there, rodeo girl."

"You, too, Daddy. And Lily was just fab, don't you think?"

"'Just fab,'" he echoed with a groan. "You've been spending too much time with those college girls who volunteer over at the rescue center."

Giggling, she squirmed out of his grasp and bolted for the back door. Through the open kitchen window, he caught the scent of what smelled like a fresh batch of his mother's secret-recipe snickerdoodles.

That left him alone with Lily for the first time since they'd arranged their unlikely partnership. Figuring he owed her a thank-you for her help, Mike swiveled to face her, intending to say something about how well things had gone. Then she smiled at him, and any coherent thought he might have shared with her went straight out of his head.

Coming down through the leaves stretching out overhead, the late-afternoon sunlight picked up a subtle pattern of lighter blue in her eyes, making them look like stars. He was standing close enough to pick up the fragrance of roses mixed with saddle oil, and he couldn't help thinking the unique mixture of class and country suited her perfectly.

Well aware that he was gawking at her like a teenager with a crippling case of puppy love, he struggled to knock his brain back into gear.

With her usual impeccable timing, she broke the silence. "It's getting late, and I've got some paperwork to do, so I should go. Thanks so much for today, Mike. I had a great time."

"Yeah, me, too."

Flashing him another of her brilliant smiles, she climbed into her car and headed up the gravel driveway to the main road. He kept his eyes on the cheery convertible until it disappeared around the bend that led to town, and for a while longer after that. He didn't know what had happened to him, or when, but there was no point in denying it. Every time he and Lily said goodbye, he found himself looking forward to the next time he'd see her.

Smitten, his father would have called it,

Mike acknowledged with a sigh. The trouble was, much as he'd like to dive in and see what might happen between the pretty teacher and him, he didn't have room in his life for anyone right now. Beyond that, Abby was his first priority, and he couldn't risk having her get attached to someone only to be left behind again.

That should have ended the whole issue for him, he thought as he trudged up the porch steps. But it didn't. And for the life of him, he didn't know what to do about it.

It was the last Wednesday of the school year, and Lily was making the rounds of her classroom when she noticed an anxious face framed in the window of her door. Seeing that it was the principal, Mr. Allen, she held up her index finger for him to wait a minute and did a quick assessment of her students' progress.

"Those letters look much better today, Frankie," she praised one boy hard at work on his alphabet. "Would you like to write them up on the smart board for us later?"

His plump cheeks broke into a huge grin. "Yes, ma'am."

Patting his shoulder, she moved past the table and met the principal out in the hallway. "Good morning, Mr. Allen. What can I do for you?"

"I'm hoping you can get me out of a jam," he replied in a panicky voice. "One of the first-grade classes is putting on their play this afternoon. The parents are on their way, and the teacher who's supposed to be in charge just called from the hospital. Her husband broke his leg at work, and she's going to be out the rest of the day."

"Can't someone else step in? I don't know the first thing about this play."

"The room moms have the costumes, props and music under control. I just need someone to keep the kids in line while they're waiting backstage. Eighteen hyper seven-year-olds are more than the volunteers can manage on their own."

Apparently, she'd gotten a bit of a reputation during her brief time in Oaks Crossing, she realized with a mental sigh. Lily St. George: Kid Wrangler. Everyone had a talent, she supposed, and stepping in to help out this way would certainly look good in the teamwork section of her professional assessment. Still, she wasn't sure what to do about her own class. Then a solution occurred to her, and she said, "I'm happy to pitch in, as long as my students can come watch the show. It'll be a nice surprise for them."

"Fine. And thank you very much. You've

saved me the trouble of canceling the performance and disappointing the kids and their families." After shaking her hand, he hurried back down the hall even as the loudspeaker started paging him about a crisis in the cafeteria.

When she filled her class in on their change in plans for this morning, they cheered with the kind of enthusiasm she adored in young children. At this age, it was all or nothing, and she often wished it was possible for people to hold on to that attitude as they grew up. Everyday worries and responsibilities had a way of eroding that optimistic view of the world, which in her opinion was a real shame. It was one of the big reasons why she'd chosen to become a teacher over any other career. Being with children all day helped her put life's ups and downs in their proper perspective.

She kept an eye on the clock and interrupted their lesson on plants at a good stopping point. "Okay, let's get ready to go to the auditorium. Quietly," she reminded them with a finger over her lips. "Other students are still working in their classrooms, and we don't want to distract them."

They gathered near the door in as orderly a fashion as could be expected from a group of excited kindergarteners, and she rewarded them with a smile before leading them into the hallway. Once she got them all seated near the back of the audience, Principal Allen hustled over, tie flapping over the shoulder of his suit jacket.

"Thanks again, Miss St. George. I'll stay and watch them for you while you're backstage." Glancing over the little group, he gave them a somber warning look. "This is a treat for you, and I expect you to be on your best behavior."

His announcement was met with a chorus of muted "yes, sirs," and Lily had to smother a grin. After working as a teacher's aide in larger city schools, she was still getting used to the humble, old-fashioned manners these children's parents had obviously drummed into their heads. That innate respect for authority had certainly made her first solo teaching job easier, she thought as she hustled around the stage and up the steps that led into the wings.

Back here, everything was chaos. The carrot's frothy green cap had somehow landed on the head of a plump tomato, and the corn's costume had twisted sideways so that only half of her face was visible.

The two moms couldn't have looked more different if they'd tried. One looked as if she was ready to pull out every last strand of her disheveled hair. The other calmly moved from child to child, fixing costumes and offering an encouraging smile to each actor before moving on. Given a choice, Lily opted to approach the composed, efficient mother first.

"The cavalry's here," she said, putting out her hand. "Lily St. George."

"Erin Kinley. I've heard a lot about you the past couple of weeks," she added with a mischievous grin. "From Abby and Mom, of course. Mike hasn't said a word."

How flattering. Then again, the trainer's reticence wasn't a topic she had time to ponder right now, so she moved past it. "How can I help?"

"These guys are done." Erin pointed to a bundle of veggies and fruits to her right. "If you get them lined up by size, I'll send you more when they're ready. Are you all set, Parker?"

A slender boy with puppy-dog brown eyes nodded somberly, the cluster of pea pods on his cap bobbing with the motion. "Yes, ma'am."

Concern passed over Erin's face, but she quickly drowned it in a smile. "That's my boy. You can help Miss St. George."

Their overly polite exchange struck Lily as odd, but she realized it was not only none of her business, she was too busy for mysteries right now.

"Sounds good. This way, crops." Holding out her arm, she motioned for Parker and the others to follow her from the crowded dressing area.

Five hectic minutes later, the woman at the piano started playing a chipper march, and the show was under way. Lily wasn't sure if she was supposed to go into the audience or hang back to corral the actors as they left the stage. Since Erin was the only adult not scurrying around or feeding the kids lines, Lily approached her and whispered her name.

"Would you like me to stick around?"

"No, we're good. Thanks for being so great with Parker. I guess you noticed he has a tough time dealing with grown-ups."

Erin paused but didn't turn away, and Lily got the feeling there was more she wanted to say. Waiting patiently, Lily kept her expression as open as possible.

Finally, Erin said, "He's been in the foster system for two years now. When I first met him six months ago, he couldn't even look at me without flinching. Now that I'm his foster mom, we're making some progress."

Stunned by the revelation, Lily frowned.

"What kind of monster could even think of hurting that wonderful little boy?"

"Someone who'd better pray they never meet up with me, that's for sure."

Fury crackled in hazel eyes that reminded Lily of Maggie's, and she was impressed by Erin's spirit—and her generosity. Taking in someone else's child couldn't be easy. Taking in one who'd been abused must be exponentially harder. Apparently, Mike wasn't the only Kinley with a willingness to tackle difficult situations.

"Anyway, I just wanted you to know," Erin continued in a whisper. "In case someone in town mentions it to you. Not everyone around here approves of a single woman taking in a troubled young boy, and you know how folks can exaggerate when they get to talking."

Boy, did she, Lily mused with a quiet sigh. Of course, she was used to people gossiping about her famous and somewhat notorious family, not an innocent child who couldn't help the circumstances he'd been born into. She patted Erin's arm reassuringly. "I appreciate that, but I always make up my own mind about people. Especially nice ones who give up their morning to shoehorn a bunch of squirming kids into food costumes."

They traded smiles, and Lily left the wings

feeling hopeful that she'd made a new friend. She'd left her social circle behind in Louisville, and at any rate most of them were completely baffled by the direction she'd chosen to take. The few college acquaintances she'd managed to keep in touch with were scattered up and down the East Coast, immersed in their own demanding lives. Much as she enjoyed her job, being new in town had made for some lonely evenings and weekends.

That was the main reason she'd volunteered to help with Gallimore's new riding school. Because she refused to take any more money from her indulgent grandfather, the extra income would definitely come in handy. But to her, time at the farm was absolutely priceless.

As if on cue from some unseen director, Mike caught her eye from his seat on the end of a row near the back. Abby was perched on his lap, and he slid down to make a spot for Lily beside them. A quick glance at her class showed them totally engrossed in the humorous scene, and the principal gave her a subtle thumbs-up. Deciding things were under control, she sat down to enjoy the play.

"I'm surprised to see you here," she murmured without taking her eyes from the stage.

"It's for Parker."

He didn't say anything more, but there was

a fondness beneath the brusque tone that gave him away. Then she noticed Maggie sitting to his right, and a thinner version of Mike beside her. Erin's commitment to Parker was touching enough on its own. That her family shared it was something far beyond Lily's experience.

People she knew took care of their own, maybe donated some time or money to an important charity here and there. That anyone would step up and form a family around a lost little boy absolutely amazed her, but she knew if she made a fuss about it, Mike would just shrug it off. So she simply said, "He's the pea pods."

Mike chuckled. "Yeah, he was complaining about that the other day. He hates peas."

"Who doesn't?"

The two of them grinned at each other, and fortunately the first song ended in a round of applause that covered the noise they were making. Through the rest of the presentation, they kept quiet, but a few times Lily noticed Mike's eyes flick over to her. She couldn't imagine why, but she was just vain enough to admit it was nice to know she'd gotten the attention of the handsome horse trainer. Even if he hadn't bothered to mention her to his sister.

Not that she'd do anything to encourage his interest, of course. But losing Chad Wellington to her younger sister had dealt a severe blow to Lily's confidence, not to mention her ego. Their whirlwind romance and lavish wedding hadn't helped any.

Lily's brooding came to an abrupt halt when she realized Mike had leaned closer to her. He smelled of fresh hay and soap, a down-to-earth kind of scent most men she knew avoided at all costs. It went along with hard work, and she couldn't help thinking no cologne company could have come up with anything that suited him any better.

"I think we're done," he murmured into her ear.

When she registered the fact that the lights had come up and the audience was clapping, she hastily joined in. What on earth was wrong with her? The play was over, and she'd hardly taken in a single line. Knowing that part of her distraction was the father of one of her students only reinforced her determination to keep things between them strictly professional. Becoming a full-fledged teacher was too important to her to risk it for anything. Or anyone.

Lily was gathering her class together to return to their room when Erin and Parker approached them. While many of the actors had shed their costumes, Parker still wore his, even though he was obviously miserable being dressed as his least favorite vegetable.

"Lemme help you with that," Mike teased, tipping the brim of the boy's cap so it popped off and into Mike's hand. "Better?"

Parker responded with a timid half grin, but it was the most emotion Lily had seen from him so far. "Thanks."

"Anytime, sport. Next time my sister volunteers you for something, tell 'em you want to be something cool, okay?"

The boy gazed up at Mike with wide eyes, clearly intrigued. "Like what?"

"Like a wolf or a lion."

"It was a play about eating right and staying healthy," Erin reminded him curtly.

"Steak, then. Everyone likes steak," he added with a wink for her foster son.

Parker's grin deepened, and he nodded. "I'll remember."

"Good man." When Maggie tapped Mike's shoulder, he gazed down at her with a patient look. "What?"

"Aren't you going to introduce Lily to your brother?"

"Don't hold your breath, Mom," the tall man warned with a laugh. "Don't forget, the last time he did that, I ran off with his prom date."

Mike made a face back at him, then turned

to Lily. "Lily St. George, this is my pain-in-the-neck little brother Drew. Not to be confused with my other pain-in-the-neck little brother Josh. Where is he, anyway?"

"Some kind of haying emergency," Drew replied smoothly before turning a megawatt smile on Lily. "I've been hearing all kinds of great things about you, Miss St. George. It's great to finally meet you and find out they're all true."

As she shook the hand he offered her, she couldn't help thinking how incredibly different he and Mike were. Unlike his older brother, Drew seemed to have inherited a large helping of his father's Irish charm. She wasn't sure why, but while they chatted, it dawned on her that for some odd reason, she preferred Mike's honest gruffness to his brother's well-rehearsed approach.

After what felt like a polite amount of time, she said, "Well, it's time for us to get back to class. It was nice meeting you."

"I'm always out at the farm," Drew said with a practiced version of Mike's creaky grin. "We'll be seeing plenty of each other over the summer, I'm sure."

"I'll look forward to that," she replied, grasping Abby's hand and looking over her head to make sure the rest of the kids were ready to go. "Goodbye."

As she led them toward the open rear doors, out of the corner of her eye she caught a glimpse of Mike standing apart from his family, arms folded while he glowered mercilessly at Drew. They were locked in what appeared to be a very intense discussion, and from what she could see, Mike was doing most of the talking. Growling, probably.

Lily had no idea what that could be about, and she firmly put the image from her mind. She had her hands full with a gaggle of restless students and a lesson on photosynthesis to finish explaining in as simple terms as possible. The last thing she needed was to get distracted by a spat between the Kinley men.

Chapter Five

Mike was still stewing over his confrontation with Drew earlier when he noticed a top-heavy hay wagon coming in from the back field. Knowing he'd be needed to help unload the fresh bales, Mike tossed the rag he'd been using to clean saddles aside and strode through the end door toward the hay barn. He got there just as Josh pulled the tractor inside and was surprised to find Drew sprawled out on the back of the wagon, a sun-bleached Cincinnati Reds baseball cap over his eyes.

"What're you doing here?" Mike demanded. "I thought you were replacing those busted rails on the south fence line today."

The moron didn't even move, just swiveled his head to peer at Mike from under the brim of his hat. "I was until I saw Josh heading in. I figured he'd like a hand, so I flagged him down and he gave me a ride. What's up with you?"

"Oh, I don't know. Maybe I'm gettin' tired of bein' the only one around here who actually does what he says he's gonna do."

"Whoa, now," Josh teased, "you'd best let up on that Western drawl. Your cowboy's showing."

"I didn't ask you."

"No, you didn't," his easygoing baby brother agreed with an infuriating grin that clearly said he wasn't afraid of Mike anymore. "Just seemed like a good place to jump in and keep you two roosters apart."

Apparently born to be the peacemaker in the family, nothing ever seemed to trouble Josh for longer than it took him to conjure up a smile. Then again, he could afford to be that way. By the time a problem came to him, Mike had usually solved it himself. He'd give anything to be that carefree, he groused silently. But as the oldest, he didn't have that luxury.

"It's my fault Mike's feathers are all ruffled," Drew told Josh as he jumped down from the wagon. "I was messing with him at Parker's thing this morning."

"Oh, man," Josh groaned. "What'd you do now?"

"Nothing much. Said hello to Abby's pretty new teacher is all."

Gasping melodramatically, Josh grabbed Mike's shoulders firmly. "I know he stepped over the line, but you've gotta go easy on him. He's an idiot with more ego than sense."

"And Mom's favorite," the idiot in question chimed in, clearly enjoying himself.

Mike shook himself loose and forced a laugh. "I couldn't care less who he talks to. I'm just mad 'cause he wasn't repairing that fence like he said he would. We need to rotate the boarders onto that pasture soon so the front one can recover in time for fall."

His brothers fixed him with a pair of doubtful looks, and he ground his teeth to keep from yelling again.

"Couldn't blame him for being jealous over Lily," Drew went on, pointedly excluding Mike from the discussion. "She's a real sweetheart, even if she doesn't have the best taste in men."

"What makes you say that?" Josh asked.

"She obviously didn't care much for me, but she hung on his—" he pointed at Mike "—every word. Not to mention, Mom was telling me Lily agreed to help him give riding lessons to kids this summer, and she only wants half of her share of the profits. Can't imagine why she'd do it unless something about it appeals to her more than money."

Josh sighed. "Some folks do things just to be nice, y'know."

"No woman I ever met does anything out of the goodness of her heart. There's always something in it for them."

The cynical comment effectively ended their argument, and Mike felt a twinge of sympathy for Drew and his gloomy perspective. He understood better than most that when you'd been kicked by a woman one too many times, it was tough to believe they weren't all out to get you. He was well aware that Dana's vanishing act had left him more than a little sour on women himself. In spite of the fact that he and Drew rarely saw eye to eye, he could relate.

"It doesn't matter much, 'cause I've got no plans to get involved with someone I'm in business with," he announced in a reasonable tone. "Now, can we cut the nonsense and get this load stashed so Josh can get another one baled before that storm comes in?"

In unison, they said, "Sure," and the conversation swung onto a much safer topic: Cincinnati's prospects for getting to the World Series this year. While they batted opinions around, they quickly fell into a rhythm with Mike sliding bales to Drew, who tossed them into the hayloft, where Josh stacked them like huge bricks.

Neither of them mentioned Lily again, but Mike knew his declaration hadn't done much to divert their suspicions. If anything, it had made him sound as if he was covering the truth with a plausible lie to avoid admitting his true feelings.

Then again, he thought as he clambered over to the next pile of bales, how he really felt about Lily St. George was a mystery even to him. He hadn't expected to run into her this morning, and when she showed up at Parker's play, he was ridiculously happy to see her. Normally, he wasn't a big fan of surprises, but that one had made his day. If she hadn't excused herself to take her class back to their room, he'd have gladly stood there talking with her for as long as she wanted him to stay. He wasn't sure what that meant, but it was for real, and he definitely wasn't crazy about where his foolish heart was leading him.

The last time he followed it, he ended up divorced and raising a child on his own. That kind of experience didn't exactly inspire him to have much confidence in women, and Mike wasn't about to make the same mistake again.

When Lily pulled into Gallimore Stables Friday afternoon, she was met in the turn-around by a bouncing Abby Kinley. Though she knew she shouldn't favor any of her students over the others, the bubbly little girl was quickly becoming one of her favorites. Her cheery personality was such a contrast to her more reserved father, Lily couldn't help wondering if Abby took after her mother.

Absent mother, she added with a frown. Who could abandon this adorable child? she wondered as she stepped from her car. The woman must either hate Mike with a passion or have a heart of stone. Maybe both. Whatever the reason, Lily hoped she never had to deal with the woman in person. Chances were, it wouldn't go well for either of them.

"Hi, Lily!" the girl greeted her exuberantly, clearly delighted by having permission to call an adult by her first name. "Are you ready for your lesson?"

In reply, Lily held out one properly booted foot, and Abby laughed. "Oh, good. Daddy hates it when people forget stuff he told them."

"I can't blame him for that." A tall shadow appeared to her left, and she was glad she'd said something nice about him. Angling her head to look over at him, she smiled. "How's your day going so far?"

"Y'know how it is, little good, little bad."

"It's way better now that you're here," Abby chirped brightly. "Right, Daddy?"

"Right." The corner of his mouth quirked with a grin, and Lily got the feeling he was about to say something else. Apparently, he changed his mind, because he stepped back and motioned them to go ahead of him. "Shall we?"

Lily's second lesson on Gideon went much better, now that she was more familiar with the hulking Belgian and could trust his calm, gentle demeanor. He was still a giant compared to her, but in her mind his personality trumped the size difference that had intimidated her so much only a short while ago.

Bred for hauling things much heavier than her, he moved with a powerful grace that humbled her when she realized he was graciously allowing her to guide his steps. The ground beneath his hooves shook when he trotted, but her ride was as smooth as silk. Knowing he'd had such a troubled past before coming to Gallimore only made her more fond of him.

When Mike suggested they take a break, she reined the gelding to the middle of the riding ring and patted his shaggy neck. "He's magnificent, isn't he?"

"Don't be giving him a big head now. The last thing I need on this farm is another diva."

Lily was about to ask Mike what he meant by that when a commotion erupted outside one of the barns. Looking over, she saw a horse trailer parked there, rocking back and forth as if there was a prize fight going on inside. The banging and shouting was terrifying enough, but then Drew came flying out the back, landing on the ground in a motionless heap.

"Stay here," Mike ordered. Then he vaulted over the top fence rail and took off running.

By the time Mike reached the trailer, Drew had recovered from his violent flight enough to push up on his hands and knees. Shaking his head, he squinted into the shadowed interior. Apparently, he didn't like what he saw, because he scrambled off to the side like a crab fleeing a diving seagull. Mike knew what that meant, and he hollered, "Open the side door!"

No sooner had Drew done that than a panicked blur of copper crashed through the half-open hatch and swayed on legs that were covered in fresh gashes. Once the horse had regained his balance, he bolted down the driveway, headed for the nearest patch of open grass. Which Mike just happened to be blocking.

Holding his arms out wide, he braced his legs shoulder-width apart and held his ground. He had grown up around horses, and his father had taught him from childhood that they were flight animals and wouldn't bowl you over unless they were caught up in a stamped-ing herd and had no other choice.

Mike was counting on that instinct right now. The horse barreled close enough for Mike to recognize it as a stallion, and despite the imminent danger he was probably in, he summoned his calmest tone. "Whoa, now. No one's hurting you, boy."

The terrified animal's eyes nearly popped out of its head, and he slid to a halt about a yard in front of Mike. His flanks heaved with quick breaths, and he eyed Mike with what he could only describe as fascination.

Then, as Drew and a nervous-looking groom cautiously edged closer, the Thoroughbred covered the last few steps between them and rested his head on Mike's shoulder with a deep, heart-wrenching sigh.

The trusting gesture triggered an old memory, and Mike wrapped his arms around the horse's tense, sweaty neck. "Hey there, Chance. It's good to see you, too."

"I'll be," Drew muttered, still out of breath. "Things were so hectic at the track, I didn't recognize him."

"This is our killer horse?" Mike asked, reaching from behind to rub the sorrel's forehead in a comforting motion. "You've gotta be kidding me."

"No lie," his younger brother confirmed. "They retired him last fall and have been trying to retrain him for riding. He's been nothing but trouble all season, but they thought they'd gotten a handle on it. Out of the blue, he went berserk the other day and put a trainer and two vet techs in the hospital. The owner said he couldn't take any more risks, so it was here or the slaughterhouse."

Mike's gut tightened at the thought of this beautiful creature being put down because no one could be bothered to find out what was wrong with him. Circling the horse, he stopped so they were face-to-face and looked directly into those dark, intelligent eyes. There wasn't a trace of the crazed animal he'd seen earlier, and he simply couldn't believe his threatening tantrum had cropped up all on its own.

"Did he seem okay when you picked him up?" he asked Drew.

"Yeah, but the vet had sedated him to make sure we'd all be safe. Like I said, they've been having a lot of trouble with him."

"Then what happened?"

While he listened to the uneventful report, Mike went over the former racehorse inch by inch, searching for a sign of what was bothering him. Nothing stood out, and he ended up back in front of the horse, totally baffled.

"He went on the trailer fine," Drew finished with a frown. "When we untied him and tried to back him out, he went bananas."

Fresh out of ideas, Mike finally shrugged. "Well, he seems okay now. How 'bout you?"

"I'll live." Clearly unfazed by the whole thing, he grinned. "Mostly it's my pride that's bruised."

"Next time, open the side door first so you can dive out if you need to. That's what it's for."

"Right."

Mike really hated being the sensible one. It was always Dad's responsibility to run the checklist when they were transporting horses, making sure neither man nor beast got hurt in the process. But he was gone now, and now that Mike was running the farm, the task had fallen to him. Someone had to be in charge, Mike supposed. But there were days when he wished it didn't have to be him.

"Mike?"

Hearing Lily's voice behind him, he realized he'd forgotten all about her. Turning, he saw Gideon standing at the rail, watching the dramatic scene with his usual curiosity. "Sorry to take off like that. Are you okay?"

"Fine." Patting the Belgian's shoulder, she smiled. "Gideon took good care of me. Which is fortunate, because I don't think I can get down from here on my own."

Her wry comment blew off most of the tension he'd been feeling, and he chuckled. "Just let me get this guy settled and I'll give you a hand."

"No rush." Winging a glance around the rolling acres surrounding them, she came back to him with a smile. "I really like the view from up here."

"I'd be more than happy to help her," Drew offered smoothly.

Mike glared at him, and he backed away, hands in the air. "Never mind."

As Drew strolled back toward the trailer, laughter trailed behind him. Mike had no clue what was so funny, and he turned to Chance with a grimace. "Any clue what that was all about?"

The horse blinked at him, and Mike shook his head at his own foolishness. With the lead rope slack between them, he led their latest acquisition into what he called the Troublemaker Barn. It had large box stalls and a wide-open feel that seemed to calm even the most squirrelly horses. He was hoping it would do the same for its latest tenant.

He wasn't the least bit surprised when he heard another set of hooves clopping along behind them. Glancing back, he saw Lily and Gideon on the other side of the fence, shadowing him.

"It wasn't my idea," Lily informed him. "Gideon wants to see what's going on."

"Actually, that's cool. He's so mellow, we stable him with head cases when they first get here."

"Head cases?" she echoed with a quizzical look. "You mean there are more like him?"

"Way worse, actually. Some horses do great at the track and then retire to pleasure riding without a hitch. Some develop nasty habits and need retraining to be safe enough for regular folks to ride. That's my main job here, but we don't get enough contracts like that yet, so I have to do other things to make up the difference."

"This horse recognized you," she commented in a thoughtful tone. "How come?"

"He was born here, and his owner hired Dad to train him for the track. Back then I was his assistant, so Chance must've remembered me."

"That must be why he didn't hurt you. He could have mowed you down and kept right on going, but he didn't."

"Most horses won't do that to people even when they can. It's not in their nature."

"That's good to know," she acknowledged with a nod. "It might come in handy someday."

Surprised by the comment, he stopped and faced her. "So even after all the excitement today, you're planning to come back?"

"Oh, absolutely." Angling her head out to the side, she asked Gideon, "Is that okay with you?"

He snuffled a response, and she laughed. "I think he really does understand what we're saying to him."

"Horses are smarter than most folks give 'em credit for."

"I can relate to that."

Mike didn't have the first clue how to respond, so he wisely kept his mouth shut and slid open the stable's end door before letting Gideon in her other side. The horses followed him through, and he closed the door behind them, just to be on the safe side. Chance made a beeline for a stall that held a stray bucket of oats, so Mike let him go and bolted the sturdy door to keep him inside. He'd had enough excitement for one day.

"You come down the same way you went up," he told Lily as he reached for Gideon's reins. "Just in reverse."

"That makes sense. Do you want me to stay and help you get things put away?"

Considering the much-too-personal way he was starting to view his new student, he figured it was best if she went home. "That's okay. I can handle it."

"All right. Here I come."

When she'd swiveled into position, he grasped her around the waist and lifted her to the ground. She landed closer to him than he'd anticipated, and he caught a whiff of something new: magnolia perfume mixed with saddle soap. It was an odd combination, but like the beat-up boots she'd taken a shine to, the scent seemed to fit her perfectly.

Rattled by his reaction to her, he firmly reined in the errant thought and took a large step back. He thought he was doing well until she smiled up at him.

"Thanks for making time for me today," she said. "I know you were busy around here."

"No problem. Sorry it wasn't much of a lesson."

The sweet smile warmed to something he didn't quite understand. And wasn't sure he wanted to.

"Actually, I learned a lot." Apparently, his clueless look got through, and she went on. "About you."

"Yeah? Like what?"

"That you don't hesitate to put yourself in

danger to help a thousand-pound animal when they're in trouble. I think that kind of thing says a lot about a person, don't you?"

"I guess so," he hedged, feeling awkward and proud at the same time. He wasn't used to being praised for simply being himself. Usually, he got the opposite. "Never really thought about it."

"Someone like that is just the person I want teaching me how to ride. I know we said we'd do my lessons on Fridays, but I feel like I need a little more work right now. Do you think you can work me into your schedule again soon?"

"How 'bout Monday at four?" he heard himself ask, cringing at the eager tone in his voice. He didn't normally react to anyone that way, and he wasn't thrilled to be doing it now. Since he couldn't take it back, he did his best to look as if seeing her again that soon didn't matter all that much one way or the other.

"I'll be here with my boots on."

"Sounds good. By the way, could you not mention the excitement to my mom? There's really nothing for her to be concerned about, but if she finds out about it, she'll hassle me to death."

"What excitement?" Lily teased, giving him a cute wink.

Patting his arm in a friendly gesture, she

dropped a kiss on Gideon's cheek and headed for the exit. As Mike watched her stroll down the driveway toward her car, a furry head bumped his arm.

"I don't know about her, boy. Whattya think?"

He got a whooshing noise in reply and couldn't help chuckling at the horse's bang-on response. "Yeah, I guess that pretty much sums it up."

Chapter Six

Sunday morning dawned bright and beautiful, and Lily couldn't help smiling as she took in the view from the tiny porch outside her studio apartment. Sitting on the single wooden step, she sipped her coffee while the sleepy village around her seemed to yawn and wake itself for another day.

The gracious Victorian that had been advertising a room for rent had been a real find, she recalled as her eyes roamed the neighborhood dotted with comfortable-looking homes and well-tended gardens. There were only a few fences for containing pets such as dogs and chickens, and the other day she'd been surprised to find a glorious peacock strutting his stuff a few doors down.

Peaceful but humming with the comings and goings of everyday life, it was a far cry from

Louisville. And with each passing day, Oaks Crossing appealed to her more and more. If only she could find her way into a job somewhere in the area, she wouldn't mind staying on past the end of summer.

She heard the slap of a neighbor's screen door and looked over to find an elderly man shuffling down his front walkway with an equally elderly cocker spaniel. The owner noticed her and nodded, giving her a toothless smile that told her he'd forgotten to put his dentures in. Again. "Good morning, Mr. Farnham."

"Morning to you, too, Miss St. George. Out enjoying this lovely day?"

"I am. Are you and Lady headed down to the park in the center of all those pretty churches?"

"We are. Will we be seeing you at services today?"

Small Southern towns, she mused with another smile. In her previous life, most people she knew considered Sunday to be the day after Saturday night, designed expressly for sleeping in. Here in Oaks Crossing, she'd quickly learned that if you weren't planning to be in church, you'd better have a good excuse. "Yes, you will. I really like the way Pastor Wheaton delivers a sermon."

"Direct and to the point, just how everyone

oughta be, in my opinion. I'll leave you to your coffee, then."

"Have a good walk."

He raised a veined hand in response and continued on his way with Lady waddling along beside him. Behind her, Lily heard a tsking noise and glanced over at the open kitchen window.

"He forgets his teeth more often than not," her landlady, Beatrice Herman, chided, shaking her head while she shooed a grasshopper off the sill with a dish towel. "From what I've seen, there's not a man alive who can make it as a widower."

"Everyone does better with company, I guess. Maybe you should take him some of your famous barbecue after church," she suggested with a little grin.

"Augie Farnham? He's the same age my daddy would have been, God rest his soul." When Lily didn't respond, the woman eyed her with a long, puzzled look that gradually gave way to a laugh. "You're pulling my leg, aren't you?"

"I just suggested you take him some food. You made the romantic leap all on your own."

"At my age, it's a wonder I can still jump any distance at all. Now, if I was a young, pretty thing like you, the men'd be beating down my door."

"I don't seem to be having that problem," Lily pointed out, swallowing some more coffee. "I like it better that way. It's much easier."

"Easy, schmeasy," Bea scoffed. Her skeptical expression became pensive, and a wistful look came into her eyes. "Take it from me, dear. When you find the right man, he's worth every ounce of trouble he causes."

Drawing her head back inside, she slid the window shut and left Lily to finish her coffee in silence. *Well, quiet, anyway,* she amended her thought with a grin. All manner of birds lived in the shrubs and trees that dotted the expansive yard, and they called to one another while they dive-bombed worms in the freshly turned dirt that marked Bea's evolving vegetable garden.

Then she picked up a sound that was distinctly unbirdlike. It was a whimper so faint she couldn't be sure where it had come from, and at first she thought she'd imagined it. No, there it was again.

Listening intently, she eased off the stoop to get a better fix on its source. The cool grass tickled her bare feet, but it also muffled her steps as she moved in what she hoped was the right direction. And there, under a mulberry bush, she found the source.

A small dog cowered under the low branches, doing its best to blend into the shadows beneath the bush. Covered in mud and bits of grass, its buff-colored coat hadn't been bathed recently, which led her to think its mother might be gone. Looking around, she saw no sign of a dog or other pups.

When she came back to the pitiful orphan, she noticed its eyes were still grayish-blue. It opened its pink mouth, but it was so exhausted no sound came out. Moved by the pitiful scrap of fur, her heart lurched in sympathy. Going slowly to avoid scaring it, she reached in to take it from its damp nest and cradled it against her chest. She wasn't very large herself, but the puppy looked tiny and helpless in her arms.

"Oh, you poor little baby," she crooned, rocking the trembling animal in a calming gesture. A quick peek showed her the puppy was male, and in the space of a single heartbeat, Lily decided she had to do something to help him.

Edging toward the house, she kept up a nonsensical string of chatter to reassure her new friend. She had no idea what such a young dog would eat, so she tapped lightly on the kitchen door and waited for Bea to open it.

"What on earth?" Bea opened the towel she held and wrapped it around the bit of fur as if it was a child and handed the bundle back to Lily. "Where did you find this little darling?"

"Under a bush in the backyard. I have to get ready for church, but I wanted to make him comfortable in my bathroom in case he makes a mess. I know you don't allow pets, so I promise to find him a home as soon as possible."

"I'd love to tell you he could stay, but the last dog owner I rented to left me with a huge, expensive mess after he moved out. For now, though, I expect he'd like some watered-down milk for breakfast. Do you have any old newspapers?"

"Um, no."

"Oh, I forget," Bea replied with a chuckle. "You young folks get all your news online, don't you? I haven't read today's yet, but come on in. I think I've got some in the recycle bin under the sink."

While Lily waited in the center of the kind woman's ruthlessly immaculate kitchen, the puppy fell asleep in her arms. The trusting gesture touched her deeply, and she silently promised the tiny pup that she'd find him a wonderful, loving home so he'd never be cold or hungry again.

Bea was full of practical advice about pets,

and once she'd finished Puppy Care 101, Lily settled her fuzzy houseguest in her small bathroom with a bowl of diluted milk and a soft blanket. Seeming to realize he was finally safe, the adorable fur ball cuddled into the blanket and promptly fell back to sleep. He was so precious. She gently stroked his wrinkly forehead and plucked the worst of the grass from his coat before tapping his black button nose. After taking a few photos of him with her phone, Lily carefully stepped around him and eased the door shut behind her.

Then she quickly finished getting ready and opened the antique rosewood box where she kept Great-Grandma Katie's Bible. Tattered from many decades of love, it was almost unusable these days, but Lily still took it to church with her every Sunday. She'd never met her feisty ancestor, but carrying the antique book just felt right to her. She had a feeling Katie liked the tradition, too.

The Shepherd's Chapel was just up the street, and it was such a pleasant morning, Lily decided to walk. Built by the town's residents in the late 1800s, it was a simple, sturdy building with a modest steeple whose bell echoed in the warming air, calling the congregation to worship.

In no particular hurry, Lily strolled along

a sidewalk shaded by dark green awnings and deep porch roofs. She was still getting a feel for the quaint little town, and she paused here and there to see what the Main Street merchants had in their display windows. One showed off the latest in electronics and computers, while another was advertising half-off Kentucky Derby hats for ladies. The race had been run already this year, so she imagined they were intended for next season's Run for the Roses. She couldn't imagine planning that far ahead for a derby outfit, but she had no doubt some of her more sociable friends actually did.

Friends she hadn't heard a peep from in months, she acknowledged with a frown. She'd been so busy with her master's thesis and student teaching, it hadn't occurred to her that none of them had bothered to contact her. No emails, texts, Tweets, nothing. Apparently, her choice to forge a satisfying career of her own rather than walk herself down the aisle to become Mrs. Someone was something they simply couldn't understand.

She'd once read a quote that said following your own drummer would show you who your friends were. Now she knew exactly how true those words were.

Wading in emotions she'd rather not examine too closely, she suddenly realized she'd stopped in the middle of the sidewalk and was in danger of being late. She picked up her pace and was climbing the church steps just as the organist began playing the opening chords of their first hymn.

Lily recognized the tune for "How Great Thou Art" and smiled while she slid into a rear pew. As she opened her hymnal, she noticed the small church was nearly full, the way it had been the other two times she'd attended services here. People were beginning to recognize her, and several greeted her with nods and smiles. One in particular caught her eye this morning, and she wiggled her fingers back at a grinning Abby Kinley.

To her surprise, Abby waved her up to their row, pointing to an open spot beside her on the end. Figuring there was no harm in moving during the singing, Lily sneaked forward and settled in beside Abby.

"I saved it for you," the girl whispered, eyes glowing with pride at her foresight.

Lily whispered her thanks and glanced down the row to find the rest of the Kinleys singing along in a family chorus that blended nicely together. All except one.

Mike.

Abby must have noticed her frown, because

she motioned for Lily to lean closer. "Daddy doesn't come to church with us. Grammy says he's mad at God for taking Grampa away."

The matter-of-fact explanation sounded odd coming from such a young child, but Lily reasoned that Abby had grown up with her father's bitterness and had chosen to admire his good qualities rather than dwell on his faults. Still, it struck her as strange that he'd allow her to attend services when he'd turned his back on religion. Did that mean he still saw value in his faith? she wondered. Almost as quickly as the idea had popped into her mind, she recognized the futility of even asking the question.

Mike didn't seem to be the confiding type, so the chances of her getting an answer were remote, at best. At least he wasn't preventing Abby from embracing the faith that his family so obviously valued. While the situation wasn't ideal, Lily had to give the man credit for not sitting in church just to make a good impression on the neighbors. She knew far too many hypocrites who attended church every Sunday and then did things during the rest of the week that would have made Jesus weep.

When the hymn was finished, everyone got comfortable in their seats and looked expectantly toward the raised platform at the front of the sanctuary. There was no elegant statuary or stained glass, just an oak altar that had darkened over the years to show the detail of a grove of hand-carved oak trees that echoed the town's picturesque name.

A slender man dressed in a plain gray suit strolled over from his place in the choir section and stood at a small lectern off to the side. With no notes, he folded his hands and leaned forward on his elbows as he smiled out into the congregation. To Lily, he looked more like a grandfather about to impart some sage advice than he did a preacher.

"Good morning." The room rang with voices wishing him the same, and he continued in a folksy tone. "Y'know, I had a nice, neat sermon all prepared for today. Practiced it, had it down pat for y'all to hear. Then I looked out at this remarkable day and decided that what I had planned was all wrong." Winging a fatherly look around the crowd, he said, "That happens to the best of us sometimes. We think we're on the right path, and then something pops up in front of us to show us another way. When people say 'God works in mysterious ways,' that's what they mean."

Intellectually, Lily knew he wasn't speaking directly to her, but it certainly felt as if he was. When she glanced around her, she saw people nodding slightly, while others were frowning as if he'd hit a sore spot with them. A few, like her, appeared to be entranced by his words, as if he'd shed some light on something they'd been struggling to understand in their own lives.

Taking the lesson a bit further, for the first time she could almost view Chad breaking off their engagement as a good thing. That crushing disappointment and the embarrassment that followed it had forced her to reassess her life and admit it wasn't the one she wanted for herself. No matter how wonderful he might be, she wasn't the type of woman to exist in the shadow of her husband, following him through the maze of social obligations that had always bored her.

That was Natalie's life, and she adored it. But Lily felt there must be more out there for her, and Chad's leaving had given her the opportunity to find it. She might not be spoiled and sheltered the way she would have been as his wife, and being alone could be tough to deal with sometimes. But she was happy. Her independence was worth more to her than all the possessions in the world.

Here, in this tiny country church, she'd discovered what was truly important to her. Smiling at the vaulted ceiling, she offered up a silent "Thank you."

A warm breeze wafted through the tall window beside her, grazing her cheek with a soft touch akin to a caress. Fanciful as it was, she couldn't help feeling it was Great-Grandma Katie, reaching down from heaven to let Lily know she was proud of her.

After the service, some people filed out right away, while others hung back chatting with friends. Maggie nudged Abby, who gave her a confused look before catching on. Turning back to Lily, she asked, "Would you like to come back to the farm and have lunch with us?"

"That's very thoughtful of you, but I'll have to pass for today. I have someone waiting for me at my place." Excitement got the better of her, and she thumbed the photos icon on her phone. Spinning it, she showed Abby a shot of the napping puppy.

Letting out a delighted shriek, the girl snatched her phone away and stared at the picture with unabashed joy. "Look how little it is. Is it a boy or a girl?"

"A boy. He's so young, his eyes are barely open, but they look blue to me."

"What are you going to name him?"

"Oh, I'm not going to do that. I can't keep him, so I'll let his new owners figure out what they want to call him."

"They do that at the shelter, too," her student informed her in a very grown-up voice. "It's a good idea."

The shelter. In all the excitement, Lily had forgotten all about the farm's rescue center. But now that Abby had mentioned it, that was the perfect solution to her predicament of what to do with the little guy. Looking down at Abby, she asked, "Would you like to help me take him over there tomorrow after school?"

"Would I?" Abby echoed, sending Maggie a hopeful look. "Pleeease, Grammy?"

"I've got a better idea," the patient woman replied. "Why don't we go over to Bea's and get him, and stop in at the rescue center clinic so one of the vet techs can check him out?"

"On a Sunday?" Lily asked.

"Critters show up all the time," Maggie explained, "so there's always someone on duty. They don't earn much money, but every one of them really loves animals. Plus, they'll have all the supplies a new owner will need to take care of such a young puppy. Your little friend will be in good hands."

It sounded like an excellent plan, so Lily agreed. The pup was still asleep when they arrived, so Lily scooped him up, blanket and all, and settled him in the passenger seat. She followed Maggie to the Oaks Crossing Rescue Center and was surprised to see the older woman motioning from her car.

"Abby wants to go in with you, but I've got to get back to the house and start lunch. Would you mind if she stays here?"

"Not a bit." She smiled down at Abby, who was excitedly bouncing in place. "I could use some help picking out toys and a collar for him. He'll need something to do until he's old enough to go home with a new family."

"I'm great at shopping," the girl assured her. "Then can I hold him? I promise to be extra careful."

Giving in to Abby's affection for the cuddly armful, Lily suggested, "Why don't you take him now, while I get the door?"

"Sure." Eyes wide with the responsibility, she took the bundle as if it was made of precious crystal. The puppy's own eyes slitted open, and he let out a barely audible grumble. "Is he okay? I didn't mean to scare him."

"He's fine. That's just his way of saying hello." In truth, she had no idea if that was accurate or not, but it made sense to her and Abby seemed content with the explanation.

"You two have fun now." Waving to them, Maggie pulled around in the parking lot and headed down the lane that led to the main house.

Anxious to find out if the abandoned pup

was healthy, Lily pulled open the glass front door etched with what she recognized as the town's logo, with the words *Oaks Crossing Rescue Center* inscribed in an arch over the iconic oak trees. An old-fashioned shop's bell jingled overhead, and a door behind the reception desk opened.

Stepping through, a petite woman in pink scrubs dotted with puppies and kittens greeted them with a friendly smile. "Hey, Abby. What's shakin'?"

"This is my teacher, Miss St. George," she answered in a tone that was remarkably polite for someone who'd just been bouncing out of her patent leather shoes. "Miss St. George, this is Sierra. She works here with the animals."

Lily shook the young woman's hand and nodded at the bundle in Abby's arms. "I found a puppy under my landlady's bushes this morning. I don't know the first thing about him or how he got there, so I'm hoping you can help us make sure he's okay."

"Definitely." She came around the desk and hunkered down for a closer look. "Well, hello there, baby. What's your name?"

"He doesn't have one," Abby informed her. "But I think he looks like a Charlie."

"I think you're right about that. Are you planning to keep him?" she asked Lily. "Or were you looking for us to keep him here until he can be adopted?"

Because of Bea's rules, the option of keeping Charlie hadn't even occurred to her. Now that it had been suggested, though, she wasn't all that thrilled about leaving here without him. Folks were right when they cautioned you about taking in a stray, she realized with a smile. It sure was easy to get attached, especially with one as cute as Charlie.

Sadder than she'd anticipated, she sighed. "I can't keep him where I live, so I guess he needs to stay here until he's bigger. I do want to get him a collar and some toys, though."

"We've got plenty of both." With a gentle touch that spoke of years of practice, Sierra did a quick assessment without disturbing the puppy any more than necessary. "Other than being dirty, he looks pretty good. He's too young for shots or anything like that, but in a few weeks, he'll need to see a vet."

Something about the way she said that caught Lily's attention, and she asked, "Do you have someone here?"

"We used to, but he was on loan from a clinic and had to go back when business picked up. We're hunting for a replacement, but this place is kind of remote, and since we're a nonprofit, we can't pay what full-fledged veterinarians are used to making." Getting to her feet, she said, "I've got formula in the fridge out back, so I'll see if he's hungry and then get a cage ready for him in the baby room. Meantime, you two can check out the doggie stuff in the store. I'll cash you out when you're ready."

"You wear a lot of hats," Lily commented with honest appreciation.

The generous tech responded with a gentle smile. "Everyone who works here loves all of God's creatures. Dogs, cats, raccoons, skunks—doesn't matter to us. Our goal is to give them the best life we possibly can. If they're adoptable, we find families for them. If not, they have a forever home right here with us."

Abby had wandered into the store while they were talking, and once Sierra was gone, Lily took a business card from a countertop holder shaped like two paws. Mention of the place's nonprofit status had made an impression on her, and she tucked the card in her purse.

One thing her philanthropist of a grandfather had taught her: always be on the lookout for a way to make the world a better place. With its selfless mission and devoted staff, she couldn't imagine a more worthy cause than the Oaks Crossing Rescue Center.

On to more fun things, Lily thought as she

strolled over and met Abby in a small shop off to the side of the lobby. The canine section stocked everything from treats to squeaky toys to collars in every color of the rainbow. With the sleeping puppy cradled in her arms, Abby stood in front of the accessories, her forehead creased in concentration.

"Which one do you think Charlie would like best?" Lily asked.

"Well, he's light brown under the mud, so I think that blue one with the dog bones on it would look nice."

"Bones it is," Lily commented, hooking the collar on her finger to bring it down for him to inspect. After sniffing at it, he tentatively gnawed at the silver buckle and let out a muted grunt of approval. "That sounds like a yes to me. What else?"

Together, they chose a few toys, and Lily tore off an order form for a silver ID tag in the shape of a paw. She'd prepay the fee and leave it with Sierra so the new owners wouldn't have any excuse for not buying a name tag for their dog. By the time they were finished, Sierra returned from out back with a small milk-style carton and a reassuring smile. "We'll take good care of him, Abby, I promise. And you can come visit him anytime you want."

Despite the reassurance, Abby was clearly

reluctant to hand over her furry friend. Gazing hopefully up at Lily, she asked, "Could we bring him to the house, just for a little while?"

"Well…" Glancing at Sierra, she asked, "Is that okay?"

"Sure. I still have to get a cage ready for him anyway, so it'd actually help me out. He's probably hungry, so you take this." She dropped the chilled formula in a white paper bag printed with the center's logo and handed it over. "We have a couple of other brands, so let me know how he likes this one."

Lily thanked Sierra for all her help and held the exit door for Abby. She stowed the bag in the trunk of her car and opened the passenger door for her assistant. Very carefully, the girl slid into the seat and somehow managed to buckle the shoulder belt without disturbing Charlie. Lily had never met a child this age who was so considerate of others, and she knew even the sweetest little girl didn't come out of the box that way.

Despite the difficult situation he was forced to work with, there was no debating that Mike was doing a wonderful job raising his daughter. If he somehow managed to get her through her teenage years unscathed, she'd be a remarkable young woman.

"Abby, I want to thank you for all your help

today," she commented as she backed around and headed for the house. "I've never had a pet before, so it was nice to have an expert to give me some advice."

"You're welcome."

Her reply came in a barely audible voice, and Lily glanced over in concern. Abby was hugging her tiny armful, cheek resting on the puppy's head. The girl looked so sad, Lily's heart went out to her, even though she didn't know what was wrong.

"Are you okay?" When all she got was a shrug, she pulled off to the side of the lane and turned to give her passenger her undivided attention. "What is it, sweetie? You can tell me."

"I was just thinking how sad it is that Charlie's mommy didn't want him. I know how that feels."

Lily frowned. Mike was under the impression that because Abby was an infant when Dana left them, her mother's abandonment had no impact on her. Apparently, not remembering and not understanding were two very different things, and the intuitive girl understood the implications of being left behind all too well.

Resting a comforting hand on Abby's shoulder, Lily waited until those china-blue eyes met hers. The mournful expression she saw in them made her want to cry, and she waited a moment to be sure her voice would come without a sob in it. "Have you ever told your father how you feel about this?"

Predictably, Abby shook her head. "He doesn't like to talk about Mommy. Whenever Grammy or Aunt Erin tries, he gets mad and walks out."

"Why do you think that is?"

"He's not really mad," Abby explained with the instinctive clarity of a six-year-old. "He's sad, like I am. He loved her a lot, but after I came along she didn't want us to be a family anymore. I don't know why she didn't want me," she added, her slender shoulders heaving in a sigh.

Being the adult here, Lily felt compelled to say something, but she didn't have the slightest idea how to respond. Then she recalled something her father had told her when he had to explain to his eight-year-old daughter why the mother she loved more than anyone in the world was packing her bags. "It has absolutely nothing to do with you, sweetie. Sometimes people change when we're not looking."

Abby took a few moments to absorb that, then declared, "Grown-ups are weird."

"Tell me about it." They traded half smiles, and Lily asked, "Is there anything else?"

"No, that's it. I was just feeling bad because Charlie's mother is gone. It's a good thing you found him. Babies shouldn't be left alone with no one to take care of them."

"I agree a hundred percent," Lily commented, shifting back into gear and pulling back onto the rutted field road.

When they pulled up next to the house, Charlie finally woke up and blinked up at Abby. When she lifted the puppy to rub noses, she got a yawning whine in reply.

"I think he likes you," Lily commented, smiling over at them.

"I like him, too. Maybe when you come over to help Daddy with riding lessons, we could bring him over to watch us. Then you'd get to see him sometimes, too."

Pleased to hear the bright tone back in her voice, Lily said, "I think that's a great idea. Charlie would love that, and he could get used to being around other people and animals for when he's older."

"Babies don't know much, so you have to teach them how to behave," Abby cautioned in a knowing voice. "My friend's brother can only crawl, but he gets into everything."

"Really?" Lily got out and opened the other door for her. "Like what?"

While her passenger rattled off all the things

the little terror had munched on, smashed or all out destroyed, Lily couldn't stop laughing. She was fond of kids in general, which had led her to become a teacher in the first place. But without even trying, this endearing blend of tomboy spunk and compassion had zoomed to the top of her list.

She was really going to enjoy her summer at the farm, Lily mused with a grin. Of course, she and Mike would have to find a way to combine his brusque way of speaking with her softer approach, or their riding school would end up being an unmitigated disaster. Fortunately for him, she enjoyed a good challenge.

The very last person Mike expected to find chopping vegetables in his mother's kitchen was Lily St. George.

Barefoot and wearing a blue dress dotted with white flowers, the pretty kindergarten teacher was slicing tomatoes for a salad and chatting with his mother as if they were old friends.

"And then what did she do?" Lily asked, making it clear he'd foolishly stumbled into an old-fashioned gab session.

"Told him if he liked that car so much, he could share the garage with it." Mom chuckled while she pulled a pitcher of sweet tea from the fridge. "It seems he prefers that to being in the house with her, because he's been living in his workshop ever since."

"Boys and their toys." Giving Mike a bright grin, she added, "It's a guy thing, right?"

"I don't know about that one. Have you ever met the lady in question?" When she shook her head, he grinned back. "When you do, then we'll talk."

"Michael Adam Kinley," Mom chided, clicking her tongue in a sound he was all too familiar with. "What a thing to say."

"Hey, at least I'm not adding fuel to the gossip fire. I make it a point to leave that to the experts." Winking, he leaned in to kiss her cheek. On her best day, his mom was what you'd call a handful, but to his mind that was part of her charm. Unfortunately, she'd taught him to admire spirited women, and that had left him a divorced single father with a struggling farm to run.

Most days, thoughts like that kept spiraling downward until he was so cranky, no one wanted to talk to him. Today, instead of retreating into the living room, he settled on a stool at the breakfast bar next to a knife that was waiting for Lily to start slicing a loaf of fresh soda bread. Still steaming from the oven, it smelled fantastic, and he stuffed a hunk of it in his mouth.

"I saw that," Lily murmured, her vivid blue eyes sparkling in fun. "You left that end all ragged, you know. Your mother's going to think I can't be trusted to properly cut a loaf of bread."

This woman seemed to have a real knack for making him smile, and this time he didn't bother trying to fight it. "Just blame it on me. I'm her favorite."

"At school the other day, Drew told me he's the favorite. If I ask Josh and Erin, will they tell me the same thing?"

"Most likely. It's one of Mom's bits, and we all play along." Leaning in, he motioned Lily closer as if they were sharing some huge secret. "Truth be told, Abby beats us all, hands down. Just don't tell her that, or we won't be able to live with her."

Lily laughed, a bright, carefree sound that made him want to join in. When he did, she rewarded him with yet another incredible smile. "It's nice to hear that from you. Up to now, I've gotten the impression that you're a pretty serious guy."

Was he? While he munched his bread, Mike let his memory wander back in time, to when he was younger and didn't have a care in the world. After leaving Oaks Crossing, he'd roamed from one beautiful area of the country to another, working at ranches that offered everything from trail rides to all-out cattle drives for city folks willing to pay a hefty sum to play cowboy for a week. At the end of his trail had been New Mexico, where he met Dana and worked his way into the plum job of stable manager.

That had been his dream ever since he could remember, and the day Abby was born was still the happiest of his life. Not long after that, everything went south, and these days it was all he could do to put one foot in front of the other. For Abby's sake—and his own— he wanted nothing more than to let go of the melancholy ghosts haunting his past and be happy. He just didn't know how.

When he registered that Lily had asked him a question, he yanked his mind back into the present and met her worried gaze. "Sorry, I missed that."

"I asked if you wanted something to drink. You just wolfed down all that bread, and you must be thirsty."

He was, but he'd been so lost in his thoughts he hadn't noticed until she mentioned it. Getting up, he filled a glass with ice water from the dispenser on the fancy new fridge they'd all pitched in to buy Mom last Christmas. Then, remembering the manners she'd relentlessly pounded into his head all his life, he offered it to Lily.

"Thank you." She beamed at him, and he was glad the gesture had occurred to him.

"No problem."

Filling his own glass, he swallowed some while it dawned on him that his mother had sneaked out of the kitchen to leave him alone with Lily. Not very subtle, but apparently she assumed he needed the hint. Since leaving their visitor alone would be incredibly rude, he came up with a way to angle their conversation to her. "So, have you heard anything about openings at Oaks Crossing Elementary in the fall?"

"No," she admitted with a sigh. "And I can't keep waiting, hoping for something to turn up. When I'm not helping out with the riding school, I'll be mailing out résumés to see what I can find. This part of the state is so pretty, and the people around here have been wonderful to me. I'm hoping to be able to stay in the area, but we'll see."

"What happens if that doesn't pan out?"

"I go home and start working for my father," she confided in a discouraged voice. "It's not my favorite option, but I have to start paying my student loans this fall, so it might be my only choice."

Accustomed to her being so upbeat, the defeated tone in her voice was getting to him. Since there wasn't much else he could do, he offered what he hoped was an encouraging smile. "Just hang in there. I'm sure it'll work out the way you want it to."

"I hope you're right." Her eyes went to the framed picture of Abby's class hanging on the wall, and she added a fond smile. "I couldn't have asked for a better class to start out with. If my next one is half as good, I'll count my blessings."

She wasn't exactly preaching to him, but her phrasing made him feel itchy all of a sudden. Pulling back into himself was his usual reaction to something like that, but she'd been so open with him, he felt she deserved the same in return.

"You're probably wondering why my whole family was in church today except me."

"Abby told me." That was surprising enough. Even more so was the compassion in her eyes. "I'm sorry for the way you feel, but I understand."

He expected her to go on, but she didn't offer anything more. More than a little suspicious, he said, "Go ahead. Get your preaching in."

"I hate to disappoint you, but I'm a kindergarten teacher," she told him breezily. "My lectures all end with 'and remember to wash your hands.'"

With that, she picked up the salad she'd been tossing and carried it past him into the dining room. Stunned beyond words, Mike stood there and stared after her, trying to figure out what was wrong with him.

It seemed that no matter what they talked about, she always left him staring after her with his mouth hanging open. In his experience, when a woman did that, it was time to fish or cut bait. The trouble was, he wasn't quite ready to commit to either one, and he'd never heard of a third choice.

"Mike, come here."

Lily's voice had a laugh in it, and he strolled into the dining room to find her standing in front of the bay window that looked out over the backyard and toward the side pasture. There, framed like a painting, Abby was on her back in the grass, smiling while the little fur ball on her chest snoozed away. Shafts of sunlight broke through the leaves overhead, spotlighting them like a joyful scene in a play.

He caught movement out of the corner of his eye and had to look again to be sure he'd seen right. Grinning, he pointed off to the left. "Well, I'll be. Look at that."

Sarge, who to Mike's knowledge had never been keen on any animals other than his equine buddy, edged closer to the happy pair, ears perked with curiosity. When he reached the patch of grass where Abby was now giving the puppy a thorough belly rubbing, Sarge sat politely just out of her reach, his tail wagging hopefully while he waited. When she noticed him, she patted the ground beside her.

To Mike's complete amazement, the old terrier trotted over to her and sat, giving the rambunctious pup what Mike could only term a condescending look. Abby managed to pet them both at the same time, and after a minute of that, Sarge finally gave in and lay down beside the younger dog so Charlie could reach him better. Clearly fascinated, the puppy rolled over and stared at Sarge, his tongue hanging out of the side of his mouth in a friendly gesture.

"Oh, how cute is that?" Lily sighed, taking out her phone to snap some pictures. "I thought you said Sarge didn't like anyone other than Captain."

And you, Mike nearly added before he caught himself. It hadn't escaped him that ever since meeting Lily, the scruffy old mutt had been more sociable in general. Actually, now that he thought about it, Mike had, too. She seemed to have that effect on everyone, he mused. How she managed it, he had no clue, but he couldn't deny she had a way about her.

Being more of a keep-to-himself kind of guy, he normally couldn't relate very well to folks who were so outgoing. Lily was another story, though, and the irony wasn't lost on him. The one woman he'd met since his divorce who interested him enough to get to know her better, and he'd deemed her off-limits. Yeah, he was a genius.

"Mike?"

She was still watching the cute scene outside the window, and Mike figured it was a good thing she wasn't looking at him. If she had been, he was pretty sure the perceptive teacher would be able to guess what he'd been thinking. That was the last thing he wanted. "Yeah?"

"How would you feel about having a puppy?"

Her question just about floored him. Before he took his foolish romantic detour, he'd been thinking it would be nice for Abby to grow up with a dog of her own. "Funny that you ask, because I was thinking how we had such great dogs when we were growing up here. We always had barn hounds, but we also had a couple around the house that'd sleep on your bed at night. As I recall, we used to fight over whose turn it was."

"Let me guess," she said, spinning to face him. "You fed them your asparagus under the table."

He chuckled. "It was broccoli, but yeah, we did that a time or two. Mom pretended not to notice, but I think she knew."

"Would she mind having a dog around again? They can be a lot of work, can't they?"

"Sure, but so can kids." Then the full meaning of what she'd asked him hit home, and he could hardly believe it. "Are you telling me your family never had a dog?"

"Between the allergies and the mess, we weren't allowed to have any pets."

Her tone held a stiffness he'd never heard from her, and he regretted treading on what was obviously sensitive ground. As open and generous as she'd been so far, the stern clamping down was an unpleasant side of her that he wasn't keen to see again anytime soon. Still, he couldn't help wondering if the lack of furry friends was the only reason she'd reacted that way when he asked about her childhood.

Figuring it was none of his business, he said, "Well, around here we've got so many critters a little dirt is no problem. Mom's a total dog person, and once she gets attached to that little guy—" he pointed out the window "—Abby will have to do some serious begging to get her share of nighttimes with the puppy."

Lily rewarded him with the kind of bright smile he wouldn't mind seeing more often. "I'm so glad you feel that way. I can't keep him in my apartment, but I hated the thought of leaving him at the shelter for some stranger to take home. He's had a tough start, and I'd much rather have him living here with friends who will love him the way he deserves."

He couldn't get over how easily she'd taken to Charlie. Then again, she'd done the same with the other animals on the farm. *Not to mention himself,* he added wryly. Most folks wrote him off after a few minutes, so he didn't have much of a social circle. It took someone with an awful lot of patience to get past his well-honed defenses and actually consider him a friend.

"Puppies never stay there long," Mike assured her. "They're so cute, folks can't resist 'em."

"I'll feel better knowing he's here with you. And Abby," she added in a rush, turning away from him almost as quickly. Avoiding his eyes, she asked, "Should we go tell her the good news?"

"Sure."

It was going to make his daughter's day, he added silently as they went through the living room and headed out the door that led to the backyard. That Lily was the one who was making it happen didn't escape him, and much as he hated to admit it, he couldn't deny things had improved greatly for him since the day he met the runaway bridesmaid.

Once their summer riding school was in full swing, she'd be around the farm pretty much every day. Whether that was good or bad, he couldn't say, but he anticipated more than a few skirmishes between them. Soft-spoken as she was, he'd already learned that in her own way, she was just as stubborn as he was. Instinct warned him that if she was convinced she was right, there was precious little anyone—especially him—could do to change her mind.

Between that and the passel of kids who would be running all over the farm, it would definitely be an interesting summer. To his surprise, thinking about the chaos to come didn't bother him as much as it would have just a couple of weeks ago. In fact, he was almost looking forward to it.

Chapter Seven

When Lily arrived at the farm Monday afternoon, the front door to the farmhouse was open to let in the June breeze. An upbeat pop tune was playing somewhere inside, and she knocked on the weathered frame of the screen door. "Hello?"

After a few seconds, Maggie appeared in the hallway, a laundry basket on one hip and a bright, welcoming smile on her face. "There's no need for you to knock, Lily. You're working with Mike now, so like it or not, you're pretty much one of the family. Come on in."

One of the family, Lily echoed silently, enjoying the sound of it. The casual comfort of the rambling farm and the people who ran it appealed to her greatly, and she enjoyed knowing they considered her part of it. In her very next thought, however, she wondered if they'd be so fond of her if they knew she'd been lying to them for weeks about who she was. Eventually, she knew she'd have to come clean with them. She just had to wait for the right moment to shatter their image of her with the truth.

And then pray they could find a way to forgive her for deceiving them.

Firmly pushing that troublesome problem aside for another day, she opened the door and followed Maggie into the kitchen before setting down the two large bags she was carrying.

"Are those the T-shirts the art teacher at school made for us?" the older woman asked, enthusiasm sparkling in her eyes. "How did they turn out?"

In answer, Lily took one from the top and shook it out for her to see. Bright pink, it sported the horse-and-child-rider logo Abby had designed. Printed over the farm's name in Gallimore's signature emerald green, it looked just the way Lily had envisioned. With one small difference.

Flipping it around to show *ABBY* on the back in bold script, she grinned. "I couldn't resist. I got them with the names done for our first group, too, as a thank-you for getting us started. Sandy said if other kids want theirs customized, she can do it later on for an extra dollar. Kids love to have their name on things, so I'm assuming most of them will want it done."

"No doubt. Our girl's playing over at the neighbors' right now, but I'll make sure she gets it as soon as she comes home. Would you like something to drink?"

"Some ice water would be great." While Lily refolded Abby's shirt, Charlie waddled in from wherever he'd been, yawning big enough to make her laugh. He plopped down on the floor in an exhausted heap, resting his chin on Lily's foot with an adorable groan. "How's our little scamp doing?"

"He acts like he's been living here all his life," Maggie replied, handing her a glass before sipping from her own. "Abby's in love with him, and he obviously feels the same way about her. I have to admit I'm a bit jealous."

"Oh, Maggie," Lily teased. "Would you like a puppy, too?"

Her smile had a nostalgic tinge to it. "I guess it's just nice to have young things running around the house again. I know it sounds crazy, but sometimes I miss all the commotion we had when the kids were growing up. I even miss all the strays Erin used to sneak into her room when she thought we weren't looking."

Lily understood what the innately optimistic woman was trying not to say. One by one, as her children had grown and moved out, the farmhouse had probably seemed bigger and bigger to her. When her husband died, it must have felt like the Grand Canyon, empty and echoing with memories of their life together.

"We're going to have plenty of commotion soon," Lily reminded her brightly. "We've got fifteen students for our school so far, and our second class of five will be here Thursday afternoon. I asked all the parents when they'd like to start, and most of them said ASAP. One mom was honest enough to admit her daughter was driving them nuts, asking every day when she was going to get to wear her new cowgirl boots and learn how to ride."

"How cute is that? I'm glad she's so excited. Abby's been around horses since she was born, and sometimes I forget she's the exception, not the rule."

"It's easy to see why she loves it here. She's been telling me how psyched she is about sharing the farm with her new friends."

"I'm pleased to hear that. She was a bit on the shy side when she started kindergarten in the fall. I was more than a little worried about her at first, but Mike kept taking her to concerts and plays at school, setting up playdates, things like that. Now that she's out of her shell,

I have a tough time remembering her being any other way."

"Whenever I see them together, it's obvious what a great dad he is," Lily commented with a smile. "I'd imagine he learned some of that from his father."

"Yes, he did," Maggie replied with another melancholy smile. "He and Justin were like night and day, but there was a lot of love there in spite of their differences. Mike took his death the hardest, I think, because it happened so fast, he couldn't get back here in time to say goodbye."

Lily couldn't begin to understand what he'd gone through, trying to work and care for Abby while his family was grieving more than a thousand miles away. Even though he seemed to be cool and distant, she was beginning to see that his gruff demeanor covered a deceptively tender heart. One that loved deeply and was still struggling to navigate the unexpected curves life had thrown at him.

Like Grandpa, she realized with sudden clarity. Stalwart and resolute to a fault, both men experienced joy and pain just as intensely as people who wore their hearts on their sleeves. They just refused to show it.

Outside the window, she noticed some movement in one of the front pastures that ran alongside the road. Squinting to be sure she'd seen correctly, she asked, "Is that Chance out there?"

"Yes, it is," Maggie answered proudly. "Mike's putting him under saddle for the first time today."

Is that safe? Lily nearly blurted, then recalled that Maggie didn't know about the stallion's dangerous antics when he first arrived at the farm. She couldn't see much from where she was sitting, but she was dying to know how the handsome Thoroughbred's retraining program was going. True to his nature, Mike hadn't said a word about it to her, so she'd assumed he hadn't started yet.

Hesitant to say anything to make Maggie suspicious, she kept her tone light. "I'd like to go watch. Do you think that would be okay?"

"I can't think of a reason why not. Just be quiet and stand outside the fence rail. These horses weigh upward of a thousand pounds, and if you know what's good for you, you never want to spook one."

Lily promised to be careful and set her glass in the sink on her way outside. Pausing on the back porch, she admired yet another view of Gallimore Stables, one that most visitors probably didn't get to see.

A good-sized vegetable garden stood off to

one side, and a load of freshly washed sheets waved lazily from the clothesline. To her right was a rambling flower garden that seemed to wander through the yard with blooms of all kinds spilling onto the grass in an array of colors any landscape designer would envy. She crossed the well-used dirt lane and settled into a spot under a tree that stood outside the rail, eager to see how Mike and his troublesome pupil were doing.

While she watched, it occurred to her that in spite of the fact that he worked with horses all day long, she'd never seen Mike in a saddle. Now that she was, she couldn't help admiring the easy way he sat up there, guiding Chance with gestures so subtle, Lily couldn't pick them up even though she wasn't that far away.

"Atta boy," he praised the horse, patting his neck as he turned him into a simple figure-eight pattern. "You remember all this from the first time you learned it, don't you?"

As if in reply, Chance bobbed his magnif-icent head, making the silver buckles on his bridle jingle. He pranced a few steps to the side, but Mike chuckled and corrected him somehow. Flashing a grin at Lily, he said, "Don't look so worried. He's a guy, so he's just showing off for you."

Did she look concerned? Having seen the

very tall animal at his worst, she had to admit she wasn't all that comfortable seeing anyone on his back. Not even someone as experienced as Mike must be. Feeling silly, because clearly he knew exactly what he was doing, she forced herself to smile back. "How's he doing today?"

"Okay." In an easy motion, he reined the horse onto a new path and nudged him into a gentle trot that brought them over to the rail. "I keep thinking that he's trying too hard, though. Something's still stuck in here." Pointing to his own head, he sighed. "I've run everything at him, loud music, tractor noise, other horses. Sarge and I even took turns chasing him around the paddock. He doesn't flip out the way the previous owner was claiming, but he's definitely antsy about something. Weird stuff's going on between those furry ears of his. I just can't figure out what."

"Do you think they abused him?" Lily asked with a scowl. That anyone might harm this beautiful, intelligent creature made her absolutely furious.

Mike firmly shook his head. "I know the whole team over there, and they treat all their horses—racers and otherwise—like they're made of glass. Aside from having to sedate him for the vet and the trip here, they handled him the same way we would have. I've got no clue what's bothering him."

If there was anything Lily loved, it was a good mystery. Reaching out to rub the white strip that ran down the center of his perfectly symmetrical face, she considered what Mike had told her. If one of her students was acting in a similar way, she'd be able to ask the child what the problem was.

But, as she had learned during her first student-teaching assignment, they didn't always know how to put their emotions into words. Taking Chance's behavior as a whole, she rolled the evidence around in her mind, trying to examine it from another angle. Everyone was assuming the horse's tantrums stemmed from his temperament. What if they were being caused by something else altogether?

Eyeing the calmly grazing animal before her, an idea started coalescing in her head. "Mike?"

"Yeah?"

"Chance was retired from racing last year, right?"

"In the fall," he replied, frowning. "Why?"

"What were they training him to do next?"

"Nothing in particular that I know of. The goal was to make him into an all-around pleasure horse for someone to buy." Swinging a leg over the back of the English saddle, he landed on the ground in front of her. "What're you thinking?"

"Did he enjoy racing?"

"Loved it. Ever since he was a colt here with us, all he wanted to do was run. He's five now, and the owner said it broke his heart to take the poor guy off the track, but he didn't want Chance hurting himself in a race." Understanding glimmered in his eyes, and he grinned. "I think I follow where you're going. You think he misses racing, and that's why he gets so cranky."

Cranky wasn't quite the word she'd have used, but he'd caught her train of thought quite nicely. "What do you think he'd do if you just let him go and got out of his way?"

"I've got no idea." Cracking a mischievous little-boy grin, he suggested, "Let's find out."

He deftly removed Chance's saddle and blanket, then slipped the bridle free while the horse was in between bites of grass. Tossing the tack onto the top rail, he stepped away and folded his arms with a curious expression.

After he chomped down a few more mouthfuls, Chance perked up his ears as if he'd sensed something was different. He shook his head, then glanced over his shoulder to find he was now bareback. Then he gave Mike what

Lily could only describe as a "whassup?" kind of look.

"It's all right, buddy," Mike encouraged with a nod, pointing into the distance. "Gideon's out there. Go have some fun."

He hadn't even finished speaking before Chance wheeled on his back hooves and took off for the far end of the pasture. His sorrel coat gleaming in the sun, to Lily he looked like a bolt of copper lightning streaking through the lush bluegrass. When he caught up to his equine pal, he pulled up and tossed his head with pure joy, dancing in place as if daring Gideon to join in.

Which, to her delight, he did. The two of them bumped shoulders and then started galloping along the front fence line. Having been bred for plowing, the Belgian wasn't as fast, and Chance blew past him within a few easy strides. Then, to her astonishment, the retired racehorse slowed his pace, glancing back at his slower stablemate.

"That's incredible," she breathed in amazement. "It's like he's waiting for Gideon to catch up."

"Amazing."

Something in his tone made her look at him, and she realized he wasn't watching the horses anymore. Instead, those expressive blue eyes were fixed on her in a show of unmistakable male admiration. The heat of a blush crept up Lily's cheeks, and while she told herself it was just the sunshine, part of her suspected it was something else entirely. "D-do you mean me?"

"Yeah, I do."

His voice washed over her in a gentle drawl she'd never heard from him before. As he continued staring across the fence at her, his gaze warmed with an emotion she couldn't begin to define. After a few breathless heartbeats it vanished, and Lily convinced herself she must have imagined it.

All business again, he said, "I thought you didn't know anything about horses."

"Compared to you, I don't. But when I thought of him like a big kid with four legs, it seemed to me that he was throwing a tantrum because he wasn't getting his way. I know it's silly, but since you were stumped about what was wrong, it seemed like it was worth a shot."

"It wasn't silly at all," Mike assured her with a grin. "It was brilliant. And seeing as Abby's the only kid I've ever understood, I think it's a good thing you signed up to help me teach all these rug rats. You've got a real knack for reading kids, and you're probably gonna save my sanity."

She beamed at him, his praise settling nicely

over an ego that was still recovering from its most recent bruising. Maybe her parents and friends couldn't bring themselves to support her in an endeavor so far removed from their own, they couldn't possibly comprehend her reasons for choosing it.

But this Kentucky cowboy, who'd gradually evolved from growling bear to encouraging friend, not only understood the path she was on, he encouraged her following it. Whatever happened between them in the weeks to come, Lily knew she'd always be grateful to him for that.

Strolling along the lane that led to the barns, Lily looked around her with a contented sigh. "This is such a beautiful place. You must have loved growing up here."

"Yeah, it was great. That's why I brought Abby back east, so she could have what I did."

"She's blessed to have such a thoughtful father."

Her comment grated on his nerves, and he tried to avoid letting it show. Judging by her sudden frown, he'd missed the mark completely. He had no idea what to do next, so he waited for her to give him a hint.

Stopping in the middle of the path, she looked up at him with a stern expression.

"Mike, if we're going to be successful as partners, we need to be honest with each other. Like it or not, we'll be spending an awful lot of time together."

Oh, he'd like it fine, he corrected her silently. Probably too much. Yanking his thoughts back into line, he addressed her directly, the way she'd done with him. "I'm just not into blessings and such. God and I aren't on the best of terms these days."

Sympathy flooded her eyes, and contrary to the scolding he'd expected, she nodded slowly. "I understand. I'll be more careful about what I say."

"I didn't mean to make you feel like you have to clam up when you're around me. Religion works for some people, just not for me."

"I respect your opinion, even if I don't agree with it." Giving him an encouraging smile, she added, "We all have our challenges to face, and we handle them our own way."

Since he didn't like to dwell on the tragic circumstances that had turned him against the faith he'd been raised with, he'd never thought of it that way. But she'd given words to how he felt, and he appreciated her understanding more than he could say. It didn't seem like enough, but he dredged up a halfhearted smile. "Thanks."

"You're welcome. Now, on the phone earlier you mentioned that you wanted me to learn how to tack up Gideon so I can handle it during my next lesson. In case you haven't noticed, he's about three feet taller than me."

He welcomed the switch to a lighter topic and chuckled. "No problem. I've got a stepladder in the tack room with your name on it."

"Oh, you're hilarious." Gazing out into one of the smaller side pastures, she smiled. "It's nice to see Penny and Ginger enjoying themselves out there."

The bay sisters had their noses buried in a large swath of clover, and although he wasn't usually so inclined, he thought they'd make a pretty nice Come Visit Kentucky postcard. Then it struck him that Lily had not only remembered their names after seeing them only once, she'd been able to pick them out of a small herd of mares. In his experience, most folks weren't that observant, and he couldn't help admiring her attention to detail. For the whole time they'd been married and living on the ranch, Dana was convinced one horse looked pretty much like another. Apparently, it wasn't that women in general weren't capable of noticing the differences between individual animals. His ex-wife just hadn't bothered to try.

Detouring from the path, Lily approached the board fence that enclosed the front pasture. Resting a hand on each side of her, she swiveled her view from the horses across the rolling hill that led back toward the road. Angling a look up at him, she smiled. "I think you have the most amazing office in the whole world."

"Suits me."

"Yes, it does," she agreed with another, slightly warmer smile. He wouldn't be surprised to learn that she regularly met up with guys who did all manner of gymnastics trying to get that reaction from her. While he had no intention of doing cartwheels to impress her, he certainly wouldn't turn down one of those incredible smiles if she felt like offering it to him.

As they continued their walk, she asked, "Now that you've cracked the code, what do you think will happen to Chance?"

Mike frowned. The misunderstood stallion was covered in bruises and wounds that were in various stages of healing. While the newer ones were obviously from his harrowing trip out to Gallimore, the others were evidence that even for experienced handlers, the headstrong Thoroughbred was an ongoing challenge. Since he was fairly certain Lily didn't want to hear all that, he kept his response vague. "He's here now. We'll take good care of him."

She gave him a long, somber look and nodded her understanding. "Will you be able to teach him to trust people enough that someone besides you can ride him?"

"Maybe, maybe not," Mike replied honestly. "I'm a trainer, not a shrink. If it turns out he's not fit for another owner, he's got a home with us. That's the important thing."

"Definitely. Everyone needs a place where they feel like they belong."

The comment had a personal ring to it, as if she was looking for that kind of place herself. Before he could come up with a way to ask her about it, though, they'd arrived at the barn. She strode past the open door and made a beeline for the gate that led to the paddock where Gideon and Chance were now standing side by side, dozing in the warm afternoon sun.

"He looks so happy now," she murmured. "Like he's glad to have a friend who cares about him."

"Yeah, he and Gideon get along great."

After a moment, she glanced over at him and shook her head. "I was talking about you. He needed understanding and patience from you, and you didn't let him down."

The softness in her tone did something funky to Mike's gut, and he tried to push the uncomfortable sensation away. It receded, but he could feel it lingering around the edges of his male defenses, waiting for another opportunity to sneak in and ambush him. He didn't like the feeling, but he had no clue how to get rid of it, so he shrugged it off and motioned Lily ahead of him. "Your stepladder awaits."

"Did you really—" She stopped abruptly midsentence and stared at something in the tack room. Turning to him, she said, "That cot wasn't there before. Have you been sleeping out here?"

"Well…" he hedged, afraid she'd think he was a complete loon. Then again, he didn't normally care what people thought of him, so her opinion shouldn't matter to him. "Yeah. I was worried he might have a tough time settling in, even with Gideon stabled next to him. The past couple nights, he was pretty restless till about one, then he finally gave up and went to sleep."

Going over to the sleeping area he'd forgotten to pack away, she tapped the speakers he'd hooked up to his phone. "What kind of music does he like?"

Leave it to Lily to figure out the tunes were for the horses, he mused with a grin. "Turns out he's partial to jazz."

"And you?"

"I'm a classic rock kinda guy myself, but

I can stomach just about anything. Except opera," he clarified with a grimace. "All that caterwauling gives me a headache."

She laughed as he reached in to grab a halter from its hook. "I'm with you on that one. My favorite is country, because I like songs that tell a story."

"I'll keep that in mind. Be right back."

He wasn't two steps away when she asked, "Do you think the boys would mind if I come out with you?"

The way she referred to the horses as if they were kids made him grin. "Can't imagine they would. Just watch your feet."

"Gotcha."

He liked her can-do attitude, he realized while he slid open the bolt on a side door and led her through. Now that he thought about it, he liked her in general. Not in the plan, but there was no point in denying it. The fact that Abby adored her new teacher wasn't going to make it any easier for him to keep his distance, Mike realized. Heaving a sigh, he resigned himself to whatever was going to happen between Lily and him. Apparently, he didn't have any control over it, anyway.

When they entered the paddock, Gideon cracked open one eye, then the other as he nickered a greeting. Chance's ears perked up, and he sidled closer to his new buddy, eyeing their visitors with a sad combination of suspicion and fear. When he registered who they were, the wild look left his face, but he didn't come any closer.

"Poor baby," Lily crooned, digging in her pocket for a handful of oats Mike hadn't noticed she'd grabbed. Holding her palm out flat the way he'd taught her, she didn't move toward the skittish stallion but didn't back off, either. "Any takers?"

Gideon lumbered forward and snuffled the treat from her in one gulp. Laughing quietly, she reached up to scratch his starred forehead. With her other hand, she took more oats from her pocket and offered them to Chance. Still petting the Belgian, she talked to him but glanced at the Thoroughbred several times. He cautiously edged toward her, never taking his eyes from the treat in her dainty hand.

Then, to Mike's total surprise, Chance craned his long neck out and slurped up the oats before retreating as if nothing had happened. His behavior made Mike think of Abby when she sneaked a cookie before dinner. "Well, I'll be. He hasn't come within ten feet of anyone but Gideon and me since he got here."

"Kids and animals have always liked me," Lily confided. "It's grown-ups I have a problem with. I'd appreciate you keeping that to yourself, though."

Hearing this polished, self-assured woman admit that made him chuckle. "Your secret's safe with me."

Flashing him another knee-buckling smile, she turned to go back inside for the tacking-up lesson he'd suggested. Without prompting, Gideon followed after her like a lovelorn colt, and after a few seconds, so did Chance. Bolting the door behind them, Mike couldn't shake the feeling that something important had just happened to him.

What it was, he couldn't say, and that didn't sit right with him. For a man who prided himself on always being in control of his life, the idea of losing his grip on the reins didn't sit well with him at all.

Then again, if he had to give them up to anyone, it might not be so bad if it was Lily.

"There you go, Kayla. All fixed."

Lily stood and admired the girl's newly straightened paper hat. Made of blue paper with a gold Oaks Crossing Cougars paw print on the front, it was a decent facsimile of the more formal mortarboards the seniors would be wearing for their commencement ceremony next week. The other teachers had told her that kindergarten graduation was a fairly recent tradition for this school, but the first one had been such a hit with the kids and families alike, it was here to stay.

For the countless time, Lily found herself wishing the administrators could find a place for her in this small but vibrant district. In the month she'd been here, she'd gotten very attached to the students and staff, which had seemed all but impossible that first day when she was hard-pressed to remember everyone's name. Now that she was done with her first solo assignment, she finally felt as if she knew what she was doing in the classroom.

She'd like nothing more than to stay, but since she didn't have the clout to make that happen, she refused to dwell on it. Instead, she opened the camera app on her phone and called the kids together for some pictures. Wherever she ended up, she'd always have a warm spot in her heart for these rambunctious children. By turns they'd challenged her and amused her, but every day they had taught her more about herself and her chosen career than she could ever learn in a college lecture hall.

"Okay, now smush together a little more. Cody, stop pulling Miranda's ponytail, and, Jeremy, you need to look at me. That's it, now hold it." Snapping a couple of shots, she checked them in her viewfinder and gave them a thumbs-up. "Perfect! Nice job, gang."

There was a knock on the door, and she glanced up at the clock to see the ceremony was about ten minutes away. *Odd time for visitors,* she thought as she went to open the door. Before she had a chance to greet their guest, the entire class rushed up behind her and nearly knocked her over.

"Mrs. Howard!" their high-pitched voices shouted in unison.

Laughing, the woman reached over to steady Lily before saying, "Hello, everyone. Are you all ready for graduation?"

They chimed in with enthusiasm, shouting over each other to tell her what they thought was most important for her to hear. Out of respect for Mrs. Howard, Lily discreetly stepped back to allow them to circle around the teacher who'd guided them through most of their first year of school. Her visit was a surprise to everyone—Lily included—and Lily thought it was wonderful of her to come by. Inspiration struck, and she suggested, "I think it would be great if Mrs. Howard walked up to the stage with you to get your diplomas. What do you think?"

Another cheer greeted her proposal, and she turned to the other woman with a smile. "That sounds unanimous to me. I'll be happy to stay out front and take pictures for you."

"Not a chance," she protested with a firm shake of her head. "You came into a tough situation at the end of the year like that and handled everything beautifully. If anything, we should both go up with them."

Someone tugged on Lily's hand, and she looked down to find Abby staring up at her. "Please, Miss St. George? We want you to come with us, too."

Paper hats crinkled while the kids nodded, and she agreed with a laugh. "Well, how can I say no to that? We should leave now, but first, does anyone have to go to the bathroom?" No one spoke up, and she said, "Okay, then. Let's go graduate to first grade."

After another cheer, they more or less settled down and fell in line to head outside, where chairs were grouped around a portable platform set up in the shade of the biggest oak trees she'd ever seen. Balloons and streamers done up in the school colors of blue and gold were tied to the lower branches and wound around the stage and lectern, where Mr. Allen waited for the three kindergarten classes to arrive.

Lily spotted the Kinleys center-front, and she couldn't keep back a smile. The way the entire family gathered to celebrate together was heartwarming, and she couldn't help wondering how her life would be different now if her own family had been this close instead of scattered to the winds, following their own paths.

Pushing the negativity aside, she fell in at the rear of their line, making sure everyone kept moving once they'd waved to their delighted parents and grandparents. She'd been warned there would be a massive group photo after the ceremony. If the kids' wandering attention now was any indication of things to come, the poor photographer would definitely have her hands full.

Obviously, the principal was well aware of the students' limits, because as soon as everyone was seated, he raised his hands for quiet. "If you'll all stand and remove your hats, we'll recite the Pledge of Allegiance."

Everyone did as he asked, facing the flag that was gently billowing in the afternoon breeze. After that, he got right down to business and started calling names from the first class. Lily's crew came last, and by the time he reached them they were all squirming in their seats. Relieved that they'd made it through without a major incident, Lily watched with pride as they each walked onto the stage and accepted a parchment scroll wrapped in intertwined blue and gold ribbons.

Midway through the roster, Abby solemnly took her diploma and politely shook the principal's hand. On her way past, though, she flashed a sweet, dimpled smile at her father that would have turned the hardest heart in the world to mush. Hearing a sniffle, Lily grinned when she looked over to see Mike putting an arm around Maggie's shoulders while he leaned in to whisper something. His mother nodded, and they sat like that until the last name was read.

Considering his rough-around-the-edges exterior, Lily admired the fact that he'd allow his softer side to be seen out in public this way. Maybe there was hope for him yet.

"And now," Mr. Allen announced with a broad smile, "I'd like to introduce you to Oaks Crossing Elementary's new first-grade classes. Go, Cougars!"

Roaring back in what she assumed was the school cheer, the crowd jumped to their feet, clapping and whooping in appreciation. Lily was tempted to follow along but wasn't sure it would be considered appropriate for a teacher to do. Until she realized all the others were, and she joined in, proud to know that she'd had at least a small role in her students' success.

When it was time for the group photo, she helped corral her students into position and very happily allowed Mrs. Howard to pull her into the shot beside the kids. As the audience and graduates streamed away to check out the refreshment tables, she turned to the woman she'd met only this morning.

"Thanks so much for including me in the ceremony today," she said with heartfelt gratitude. "It really meant a lot to me."

"You're very welcome, Lily." Checking her watch, she sighed. "I hate to pose and run, but it's lunchtime for both my little ones, so I really have to get home. If you need a reference while you're applying for jobs, please let me know. You've done a wonderful job here, and I'd be delighted to write one for you."

Lily thanked her, and they hugged before Mrs. Howard left to say goodbye to the class. Alone for the first time all day, Lily took a moment to enjoy the calm before doing the mingling thing. She was confident that she was fairly well hidden in the shadows beneath a gnarled oak tree, but it didn't take long for a tall man in a cowboy hat to find her. As Mike sauntered toward her, she couldn't help admiring the easy, self-assured way he moved, as if nothing that might come his way would be too much for him to handle. Knowing what she did about his past, she knew that swagger wasn't just an image he projected to impress other people.

That was who he was.

She'd known enough men who put on one face for the world when another, less appealing one was their true self. It was refreshing to meet a guy who was himself, no matter what folks might think of him. Of course, the fact that underneath the grizzly personality beat the soft heart of a teddy bear was an unexpected bonus for anyone who was persistent enough to dig down and find it.

"So, what'd ya think?" he asked with a grin. "Pretty cute, huh?"

"Very. All Abby talked about was how proud you were going to be of her."

"Aw, that's easy. She's a great kid."

"They don't come out of the box that way," Lily reminded him, smiling back. "You're doing a fabulous job raising her."

"Thanks." His bright expression suddenly dimmed, and he muttered something awful under his breath before growling, "What is *she* doing here?"

Following his line of sight, she saw a slender woman with wavy blond hair coming toward them. It didn't take a genius to see Abby in the mysterious visitor's face, and Lily instinctively backed away. "I'll leave you two alone."

To her astonishment, he fixed a pleading look on her. "If you could stay, I'd really appreciate it. Otherwise I'm liable to do something that'll feel good now but land me in a heap of trouble later."

She waited for that wry grin, but it never materialized. So, because she didn't want anything to spoil this happy moment for him and his daughter, she nodded. "For Abby."

"Thanks."

Mike stood tensely beside her, hands shoved in his front pockets in an obvious attempt to appear nonchalant. From where Lily was standing, the carefree pose did nothing to ease the anger that was pouring off him in waves. Apparently, the woman approaching him sensed it, too, because she stopped a few feet away. "Mike."

"Dana."

He spat out her name as if it tasted bitter in his mouth, and Lily sent up a silent prayer for this awkward reunion to go as well as humanly possible.

After studying him for a few seconds, Dana turned to Lily. "I'm Dana Parsons, Abby's mother."

"Lily St. George. I was one of her teachers this year."

"Nice." Clearly uncomfortable, Dana glanced around the small clearing as if searching for something else to say. "Everyone did a good job with the ceremony."

"I'm glad you enjoyed it."

The halting conversation seemed to be wearing thin on Mike, and he snarled, "What are you doing here, D?"

"Same as you," she replied evenly. "Watching my baby graduate from kindergarten."

"She's not a baby anymore, in case you haven't noticed."

Lily slid a step closer, willing him to keep his cool. While he had every right to be furious at the intrusion, she knew he'd regret making a scene in public on his daughter's big day. Her silent advice seemed to get through to him, because he folded his arms and let out a deep sigh.

"How'd you even know about this thing?" he asked in a slightly more pleasant tone.

"I know how old she is," Dana reasoned calmly. "My boss and I were scheduled to be in Louisville on business, and I decided to make an extra stop here before we leave tomorrow. When I looked up the news on the school's website, it mentioned the kindergarten graduation was today, and it seemed like a fortunate coincidence. I thought I should be here."

"Why?" Taking an intimidating step forward, he glared unmercifully down at her. "After being MIA for the past five years, why do you even care?"

Dana's chin trembled with private emotions, but she firmed it and returned his stare with a stony one of her own. "She's my daughter, too, Mike. I have a right to be here."

Suspicion darkened his eyes, and he cocked his head like a dubious hound. "And?"

"That's all."

Any moron could see the woman was lying, and by his steely glare, Mike knew it, too. But Dana stubbornly refused to say anything more, and after several tense moments, he finally backed down.

"Fine," he gritted through clenched teeth. "But I'm warning you—stay away from my daughter, or I'll hire a lawyer who'll make you wish you had."

With that, he spun on the heel of his boot and stalked over to where his family was standing with Abby. The protective ring made Lily think of brave, determined settlers circling the wagons to fend off an attack. While she wasn't at all certain what to make of Dana's unexpected—and unwelcome—reappearance in Abby's life, one thing was abundantly clear.

Something strange was going on. And while Mike might not know exactly what his ex-wife had in mind, he was prepared to do whatever it took to keep her out.

Lily's troubling train of thought slammed to an abrupt halt when she realized Dana was now looking at her. She wasn't thrilled with the idea of entertaining this perplexing stranger, but a lifetime of social training dictated she at least be civil, so she tried to appear neutral. "Did you need something else?"

"I can just imagine what you've heard about me."

"Not much, actually," Lily replied truthfully.

Dana's blue eyes widened in shock, narrowing as she shook her head with a grimace. "I guess I shouldn't be surprised by that. When Mike finally settles down, I was hoping you'd give him a message for me."

Lily hated the sound of that, and she did her best not to whine. "Why me?"

"You're here together. I figured that meant—"

"I'm Abby's teacher," Lily reminded her politely. "Nothing more."

Dana's doubtful expression made it clear she didn't believe that for a second. To be honest, Lily wasn't sure she did, either. There was something more than simple friendship between her and the stoic rancher, but she couldn't quite define what it was.

"Anyway," the woman continued, "I'm coming back through here next week on my way home to Dallas. I'll be staying at the B and B over in Rockville, and I want to spend some time with Abby before I leave."

Hoping she sounded completely disinterested, Lily asked, "How long are you planning to stay?"

"As long as it takes. Mike's as hardheaded as they come, but he's also fair. If I'm patient, he'll work his way around to doing the right thing. Eventually," she added with a sour face.

The comment on his character sounded odd coming from the woman who'd walked out on him so long ago, and Lily couldn't tamp down her curiosity any longer. Glancing around to be sure no one was listening, she moved closer to keep their conversation private. "If I agree to give him the message, may I ask you something?"

"Sure."

"What happened with you and Mike? It seems to me that parents with a new baby would be too happy to argue about much."

"You'd think so, but no." Heaving a deep

sigh, she cast a wistful look across the lawn to where her daughter was chatting with her friends. Coming back to Lily, she went on. "Mike and I were having problems long before Abby came along. For a while she brought us closer together, but in the long run, even she wasn't enough to save our marriage. Near the end I was such a mess, I figured they'd be better off without me, so I left."

Regret laced her confession, and Lily couldn't help feeling sorry for her. Wishing there was more she could do, she said, "It took a lot of courage for you to come here."

Emotion welled in her eyes, and she frowned. "It kills me to think of how much time I've lost with Abby. Mike and I were done, but looking back I know I should've stuck around for my daughter. I really thought me leaving was best for both of us, but I was wrong. So, so wrong."

That kind of remorse couldn't be faked, Lily knew, and her compassion grew for this troubled soul who seemed so desperate to put things to rights. But this wasn't Lily's battle to fight, and there was only so much she could do. Offering a smile of encouragement, she said, "I'll give Mike your message. But as you saw, he's very protective of Abby, so beyond that, I can't promise you anything."

"I understand." Adding a watery smile,

Dana handed her a piece of paper with a number scribbled on it. "This is my cell number, in case you need to reach me. I really hope you do, because…"

Her voice trailed off before she finished her explanation, but the misery clouding her cover-model features spoke volumes. Casting another longing look at Abby, Dana squared her shoulders before turning away and slowly walking to the parking lot. She seemed to be dragging her feet, as if she could barely stand the thought of leaving without talking to her daughter.

While she processed what had just happened, Lily's mind went back to the morning she'd found a lost puppy who'd been abandoned for no discernible reason. Abby had felt an immediate kinship with Charlie, and Lily wondered how the little girl would react if she knew the mother she'd never known had traveled so far to meet her.

Lily's own childhood had been filled with mothers who came and went, never stopping to consider how their absence affected anyone else. At least Dana had come to grips with her mistake and was trying to make amends.

That was how she'd present the idea to Mike, anyway, Lily mused as she strolled over to pour herself a glass of punch. In the end, it was his decision. She just prayed he'd make the right one.

Chapter Eight

"I don't wanna talk about it, Mom."

Mike thought he'd made that point already, loudly and more than once. But he heard footsteps coming up behind him and wanted to prevent a long, tedious argument that would accomplish nothing except fanning his simmering temper into an all-out bonfire. Lifting the sledgehammer over his head, he pounded down on the fence post he was replacing. Usually manual labor was the cure for whatever ailed him, bleeding off his frustration in a flood of sweat and tiring him out so he could come up with a solution to whatever problem was confounding him.

This was different. Abby meant the world to him, and nothing was more important to him than her happiness. There was no way he'd allow Dana to worm her way back into his little girl's life, only to break Abby's heart when she decided it was time to take off again.

Once bitten, twice shy.

His father's earthy wisdom rang in his memory, bringing with it both a measure of comfort and sorrow. Of course, as usual Dad had been talking about horses, but Mike figured the advice applied just as well to women.

Except Lily. Mike appreciated the way she'd stood beside him during his unpleasant encounter with Dana. He'd almost felt Lily sending him "be nice" vibes so he wouldn't say or do anything stupid. Livid as he'd been at the time, once he calmed down, he had to admit he admired the lady's courage. It wasn't every day you came across a woman willing to save you from yourself.

"Okay, then I'll talk and you can listen."

Stunned to hear Lily's soft drawl, he whirled to find her standing behind him, a glass of sweet tea in one hand and a paper-wrapped deli sandwich in the other. Her intent was obvious, and he deflected it with a growl. "I'm not hungry, and I'm not listening."

His traitorous stomach rumbled its own opinion, and she tilted her head with a decidedly feminine smirk. "Does that mean I can talk while you eat?"

"Sure, long as you don't mention Dana."

He wiped his sweaty face on the sleeve of his grimy T-shirt, then rubbed his hands on his jeans to get the worst of the dirt off them. When he realized she hadn't responded to his comment, he groaned. "Gimme a break, Lily. The woman ambushed me in front of half the town, and I just about had to bite my tongue in half to keep things civil."

As usual, she was completely unfazed by his grumbling. She pulled herself up to sit on the new fence rail and set his snack down on the flat top of the post beside her in an unspoken invitation. Resting a hand on each side of her, she gave him the kind of patient look he figured she used on kids who needed extra time to work through a tough math problem.

She didn't say a word, but she didn't look away from him, either. Out here, surrounded by blue sky and rolling fields dotted with wildflowers, she should have looked out of place in her conservative gray slacks and pink blouse. Instead, he noticed how her eyes had deepened to the color of cornflowers, and how the wind swirled lazily through the curls in her hair.

The poetic image of her was so unlike him, he decided he must be hungrier than he thought. Out of necessity, he picked up the sandwich and took a large bite to keep from having to say anything to her. Why he was suddenly shy about talking to her, he had no idea. But his gut was telling him to keep his thoughts to himself, and he figured it was best to pay attention to that instinct.

Most women he'd known could take only so much silence, but once again, Lily proved she was made of sterner stuff. She waited for him to finish his snack and wash it down. It must've taken him ten minutes, but she didn't make a peep the entire time.

Finally, he decided enough was enough. "You can't be very comfortable sitting up there like that."

"I didn't see any alternatives."

"There's a couple stumps we haven't pulled just over the ridge here. They should work okay."

He reached up to help her down, but she drew away. "You promise to keep an open mind about what I have to say?"

"No," he replied honestly, "but I promise to hear you out. Take it or leave it."

After a moment, she relented with a sigh. "I'll take it."

With that settled, he lifted her down, being careful to keep some distance between them. Unfortunately, the uncooperative breeze kicked up at just the wrong time, sending the scent of her perfume squarely into his face. Today she was wearing a blend of magnolias and some other flowery scent he didn't recognize. It reminded him of the bouquets his mother loved to keep around the house in the summertime.

The image of Lily strolling through a blooming garden was almost more than he could stand, and he took a healthy step back, hoping to escape the unwelcome rush of sensations it had unleashed. Reminding himself that she was about to force him to confront his feelings about his ex-wife helped cool things down, but not as much as it should have.

When they were seated, he stubbornly waited for her to open the conversation. He recognized that she was trying to be helpful, but that didn't mean he was obliged to cooperate. The stony-silence routine convinced most folks to leave him be, but not this woman. In her own way, Lily was even more stubborn than he was.

"I'm sure you noticed me talking with Dana at school today," she began in a maddeningly reasonable tone. "The upshot is she's coming back here next week and wants to see Abby. She told me she's not leaving until she gets to spend some time with her daughter."

Seriously? That was the best she had? Slightly disappointed, Mike laughed derisively. "I don't think so. I'm sure she's got a job, so she has to go home when she runs out of vacation time or money. I can wait."

Lily raised an eyebrow in obvious disapproval. "That's not fair."

"Fair?" Incensed, he jumped to his feet and stalked a few feet away to get ahold of his temper. Whipping around, he glared down at Lily, who for some inexplicable reason didn't appear to be the least bit worried. "I'll tell you what's not fair. She lied about loving me and our daughter, then took off in the middle of the night with no warning and no explanation. Show me the law that says I'm expected to help her worm her way back into our lives."

Lily chewed on that for a few seconds, and he wondered how she'd respond. To be honest, he was more than a little impressed by her attempt to bring Dana some peace, whether she deserved it or not. Not many people he knew would stick their necks out so far for a stranger when there was nothing in it for them.

"May I ask you something?" she finally said. He gave a single nod, and she continued. "Do you still love Dana?"

"Not hardly."

"Do you think she still loves you?"

The innocent question prompted him to stop blustering and confront the very personal—and painful—issues he'd spent most of the past five years avoiding. But now that she'd forced him to face up to it, he sank onto the stump with a defeated sigh.

"I'm not sure she ever loved me in the first place," he confided, folding his hands and staring down at them to avoid her gaze. "When I met her, she was a beautiful mess and headed down a long, bad road. I was her ticket out of a roadhouse that paid her next to nothing."

"But you must have seen that she had the potential to be something more. I mean, you asked her to marry you."

"Seemed like a good idea at the time." Lily didn't comment on that, and he finally lifted his head to meet her eyes. In them, he saw something he seldom got from anyone: understanding. Gaining confidence from her sympathy, he went on. "I loved her, though, even more after Abby was born. For all her flaws, Dana was great with her, and it seemed like she'd finally found something that made her happy. It felt good knowing I gave that to her, that we were gonna be a family together. That's why it hurt so much when she left."

"She did more than reject you," Lily filled in the blank for him. "She walked out on the dream just when it was coming true."

The phrasing was a little mushy for him, but

she had the gist, so he nodded. "Can I tell you something no one else knows?"

"Sure."

"I really hate weddings."

To his amazement, she laughed, shaking her head while she smiled at him. "There's something we have in common. The only one I can think of that I've actually enjoyed was my sister's."

"Really? How come?"

Reaching out, she rubbed his arm with a gentle touch. "Because that's where I met you. I'd been living a quiet little life until then, and except for teaching, I was bored out of my mind. Ever since then, I've met a ton of new people, and I'm having a blast spending so much time here at the farm. A lot of that is your doing, and I really appreciate it."

"I didn't do much, really."

"You're not good at taking a compliment, are you?"

"Guess not," he allowed with a grin. "Don't get much practice."

"Maybe that's because you scare everyone away before they get a chance to see how great you are."

"Everyone but you. Why is that?"

"I work with other people's kids all day,"

she replied, eyes twinkling in fun. "I'm tough to scare."

"I get what you're trying to do, y'know, and it's not gonna work. As long as I'm breathing, Dana's not getting anywhere near my daughter. She didn't ask to be dragged into all this, and now she's old enough to get what's happening. I've got no intention of letting Dana charm her with all kinds of promises and then break her heart."

Lily eyed him thoughtfully. "Why don't you let Abby decide?"

"'Cause she's a kid who doesn't deserve to be put through something like this. What's she gonna say? 'No, Mom, I don't want anything to do with you'?"

"Is that what you'd want her to say?" Lily pressed. The nearly blank expression that came along with her question alerted him that she was trying to make a point with him. But this wasn't his first day dealing with a challenging woman, and he wasn't about to cave in to that kind of female pressure, no matter how sweetly it was packaged.

"This isn't about me," he reminded her curtly. "As a dad, I have a responsibility to protect my daughter from anything I think might hurt her."

"I hardly think this woman is dangerous.

She's finally realized what she's missed out on, and she wants to meet Abby. Where's the harm in that?"

Mike had reached the end of his patience, and he stood, pulling himself up to his full height so he loomed over her. Glaring down at her, very calmly he said, "I've made my decision, and nothing you can say will come close to changing my mind. You don't have kids, so I don't expect you to understand."

Even before he finished speaking, he regretted those last few words. Her open expression darkened into a stormy one, warning him he'd inadvertently blundered over some unseen line. Very slowly, she stood up and faced him squarely, disgust swirling through her eyes.

"I cannot believe you just said that," she said in that precise way she had when she was angry. "I thought we were friends, but now I see you have absolutely no idea who I am."

With that, she turned on her heel and marched back toward the house. She nearly ripped the door off her car in her haste to get away from him, and the trail of spitting gravel she left in her wake matched his current mood perfectly.

As he trudged over the hill and picked up his sledge, a voice in the back of his mind whispered that he'd just blown what might have been a good thing if only he'd given it a chance. Shutting off that tiny voice, he eyed the section of fence waiting for new posts and calculated that finishing it would take him the rest of the afternoon, if not longer.

Good news for him, he decided as he quickly got into a pounding rhythm. If he didn't have to talk to anyone until suppertime, that would suit him just fine.

"Boys are stupid."

Lifting her soda, Erin toasted Lily with a grin and a raised eyebrow. Sitting at a wrought-iron table outside the Oaks Café, they were by turns enjoying the warm summer evening and indulging in a little male bashing. Since the boy they were currently shredding was Erin's brother, Lily had been holding back her true feelings out of respect for her new friend's family. But since Erin had kicked open the barn door, Lily decided it was all right to air out her temper.

"Does he think I'm a complete imbecile?" she seethed, stabbing at the cherry on her sundae with her spoon. "I spend all day with those kids, and I see how parent troubles affect them. I wouldn't suggest anything if I thought it could hurt any of them even the tiniest bit."

Unfortunately, one of the things he'd said

during their tense conversation kept ringing in her ears. *She lied about loving me and our daughter.* Mike may not be the warm, fuzzy type, but he was a straightforward, honest guy whose loyalty ran so deep, he was willing to take on jobs he hated in a desperate bid to keep his family's struggling business afloat. Whenever she let herself think about how much he valued the truth, she got a sick feeling in her stomach.

Someday, she'd have to confess not only who she was, but also that she'd been lying to him all along. She feared that would be the day she lost him completely.

Erin gave her a long, pensive look, then glanced down at the straw she was twirling in her glass. "If you want my opinion, Mike's bullheadedness has nothing to do with Dana."

"Seriously?" Her companion nodded, and Lily sat back to consider other possibilities. When she came up empty, she frowned and shook her head. "What is it, then?"

"Goose. It's you."

"Okay, you've lost me. Mike and I were getting along just fine until this afternoon. Since we started the riding school, we've had plenty of disagreements, but we've always managed to find a compromise we can both live with."

"So what's different this time?"

Erin's smug attitude was starting to get on her nerves, and Lily sighed. "Look, it's been a long day and I'm not in the mood for twenty questions. If you've got something to tell me, just spit it out."

"Fine." Hazel eyes twinkling with humor, Erin grinned. "My big brother has a crush on you."

"He does not," Lily protested reflexively. "We're just friends."

"No, hon, you and I are friends. You and Mike are…something else. I'm not sure what yet, but there's definitely something going on there. Everyone else can see it, so I'm not sure why you're both fighting it so hard."

"Everyone?" Lily echoed dubiously. "Like who?"

"Abby, for one. If you look in that sketchbook of hers, she's got drawings of your wedding, complete with a carriage for the three of you to ride in after the ceremony."

In a heartbeat, Lily's anger gave way to sympathy for the adorable little girl who'd gotten it into her head that she, Mike and Lily were somehow going to be a family. She recalled similar yearnings from her own childhood, embracing each of Dad's successive wives with the hope that the new one would stay with them forever. She loved her own mother and visited her in South Carolina as frequently as their schedules would allow. In spite of their close relationship, she'd longed for someone who lived in the same house, to play pretend with her dollhouse and have tea parties with her. In all honesty, part of her still did.

She realized now that her quick connection with Abby wasn't a simple teacher-student thing. Raised primarily by their fathers, the two of them shared something important. And very personal. They both yearned for a mother who'd be there every day, listening, playing, helping with projects. Without meaning to, Lily had stepped into that role for Abby, and in the process she'd created an expectation for something that would last beyond the end of the summer.

When they'd first reconnected in Oaks Crossing, she'd made a vow to keep her distance from Mike and his engaging daughter to avoid hurting anyone. She'd failed miserably, and the result was so obvious, a six-year-old could see it.

Meeting Erin's sympathetic gaze, she sighed. "I really messed this one up, didn't I?"

"If your goal was to keep Mike in the friend zone, then yes, you did."

Her bemused tone plucked at Lily's already

frayed nerves, and she snarled, "What other goal could I possibly have?"

"I don't know." Leaning back, Erin crossed her sneakers on an empty bistro chair. "You tell me."

"Oh, be realistic," Lily shot back. "I certainly had no intention of getting serious with your brother."

"Y'know, sometimes the best things that happen are totally accidental. Look at chocolate chip cookies." Frustrated by the odd reference, Lily motioned for her to explain. "The story is that a woman didn't have enough chocolate to make the amount of cookies she wanted, so she chopped some into bits and mixed it into the dough. People loved them, and the rest is history."

"Let me get this straight. You're saying Mike and I are like chocolate chip cookies?"

"If you gave it a chance, you could be. I know he can be a pain, but he's a great guy, and he generally does the right thing, even when it's not the easiest way to go."

"Well, this time he's wrong." Deciding she had to confide in someone, Lily relayed the brief conversation she and Abby had had about Dana. "I don't care who's right or wrong. All I'm saying is Abby's a smart girl, and he should let her decide whether or not to meet her mother. If he forbids it altogether, I'm afraid it will come back to bite him when she's older."

Erin gave her a knowing look. "How old were you when you ran away to see your mom?"

Busted. This wasn't a part of her life Lily shared with many people, but since Erin had guessed the basics, she figured there was no harm in telling her the whole story. "They divorced when I was eight, and because of the lawyers, the custody-sharing nonsense for my sister and me went on for months. Then one day I'd had enough, so I took the money I got for my birthday and bought myself a bus ticket to Charleston."

"You're kidding!" When Lily shook her head, Erin high-fived her. "Good for you. How did you find your mom's place?"

"I had her address in Charleston, so I went up to a mounted policeman outside the bus station and asked him to help me. It wasn't far, and he took me there on his horse. It was really cool," she added with a nostalgic smile. "His name was Hercules."

"The cop or the horse?"

When they stopped laughing, Erin said, "So even back then you had a lot of spunk. That must be why we get along so well."

"Must be," Lily agreed, giggling like one

of her students. During their chat, her butter-scotch sundae had turned into a syrup-covered island surrounded by a moat, and she dipped up some of the yummy cream. After a few spoonfuls, she grudgingly admitted that she wasn't any closer to a solution about how to handle Mike than she'd been when she and Erin started talking. Since she was fresh out of ideas, she decided to appeal for help. "So, what should I do about Mike?"

"I'm not in the habit of giving folks advice," Erin hedged. "They usually don't like what I have to say, and it causes me no end of trouble."

That didn't surprise Lily in the least. Over the past few weeks, she'd learned that her new friend was a caring foster mother determined to give Parker the best life she could. In that same vein, she was also outspoken and stubborn. *Much like her brother,* Lily mused with a smile. They must be Kinley traits, but being from Irish stock herself, they were characteristics she could definitely appreciate. "Go ahead. I promise not to shoot the messenger."

For several moments, Erin stared at the melting ice cubes in her glass, twirling the straw through them with a somber expression. Then she appeared to make up her mind and lifted her head to gaze over at Lily. "Ordinarily, I'd say let him sweat it out and come crawling to you to apologize. But—"

"Dana walked out on him," Lily picked up the thread without hesitation. "And he never went after her."

"He claims it's because of Abby, but I've always suspected there was more to it than that. Sometimes I think he'd rather die of loneliness than risk trusting the wrong woman again."

Swirling her spoon in her sundae soup, Lily absorbed Erin's comment in silence. Lost in thought, she was vaguely aware of a car pulling up at the curb not far from their table.

"Well, I'll be," Erin breathed, making Lily turn to see what had gotten her attention.

There, standing with his back against the fender of a dark green Gallimore pickup, was Mike. Arms crossed, he was staring at them as if he was trying to decide how to handle the situation.

"Mike's never chased after anyone before," Erin told her. "He must think you're something special."

"You think so?"

"He's here, isn't he? Want me to take a picture so people will believe it?"

Laughing, Lily stood and set down enough money to cover their bill along with a generous tip. "Thanks for listening."

"Anytime. Do me a favor?"

"What's that?"

"Talk loud enough so I can hear."

"In your dreams," Lily scoffed as she headed toward Mike's truck. Behind her, she heard, "Spoilsport," but didn't bother to reply. She had more important things to think about right now.

When a rock-stubborn Irishman trailed after you for any reason at all, it was best to give him your undivided attention.

Mike had never seen that guarded look in Lily's clear blue eyes before, and he mentally kicked himself for being the one to put it there. After some sledgehammer therapy and a long shower, he'd finally calmed down enough to rethink how he'd handled things this afternoon and came to a painfully obvious conclusion.

"Lily, I'm a moron," he began, hoping that at the very least she'd give him credit for honesty.

Glancing back over her shoulder, she smirked at his little sister in some kind of female message he couldn't begin to understand. Didn't much want to, either. When that wide-open gaze settled back on him, it had a stern quality to it that made him want to squirm.

Man, she was good. Anyone misbehaving in her class must hate to see that look in her eyes.

She didn't say anything, though, just crossed her arms and stared at him with an expectant look. As the seconds ticked by, he started wondering what point she was trying to make. Then it hit him, and he said, "I'm sorry."

"For being a moron?"

That wasn't quite what he wanted to say, and he searched for a way to explain it to her. Calmly this time. "For taking out my temper on you. Seeing Dana was bad enough. Finding out she's set on meeting Abby kinda sent me over the edge." Lily tipped her head in a chiding gesture, and he chuckled at his own stupidity. "Okay, really sent me over. Happy?"

"Not exactly, but I appreciate you being up front with me. Apology accepted."

Mike let out a deep breath and sank back against the front fender in relief. He hadn't really been expecting her to understand. After the way he'd treated her, he figured the best he could hope for was that she'd listen and then send him on his miserable way.

Watching her walk away from him had been the hardest thing he'd done in a very long time. He wasn't keen on doing it again. Since he wasn't ready to tell her that just yet, he settled for, "Thanks."

"You're welcome, but next time try harder to explain how you're feeling, okay?"

"Got it."

"So," she pressed, "are you going to let Abby decide for herself?"

"She's a curious kid, so I'm pretty sure she'll want to see her mom. But I'll make sure I'm around just in case things get dicey."

"That won't be easy for you," Lily pointed out with a frown.

"No, but that's how it's gonna be, or it's not happening. Dana did things her way before, but this time Abby will know what's going on, so I'm calling the shots. If Dana doesn't like that, too bad."

Resting a hand on his arm, Lily rewarded him with a proud smile. "Abby's blessed to have such a caring man for a father."

She'd said that to him once before, and it hadn't settled well. This time, though, the idea didn't bother him at all, and he briefly wondered what had changed. Then it hit him, and he couldn't keep back a grin.

It was Lily.

Somehow, when he wasn't paying attention, she'd found her way into his heart and revived the part of him that had been shut down since his father died. Recognizing that he never could have managed that on his own, Mike was more grateful to her than he could possibly say.

Hoping to end their day on a more harmonious note, he said, "Abby's with Parker on the playground. Wanna come over?"

"Are you planning to talk to her about Dana?"

"I figure I better before I change my mind."

"I think maybe that's father-daughter business," she hedged. "I wouldn't want to be a third wheel."

"You won't."

Mike anxiously waited for her to answer. Out of necessity, over the years he'd become a very cautious man. When it came to relationships, he held on to the people who'd been in his life for years, because they were the ones he was certain would never hurt him or his daughter. In a very short time, Lily had joined his short list of trustworthy people, and even though it baffled him, he couldn't deny the truth of it.

He'd trusted this sweet-natured, feisty teacher from the very first time they met. Her sister's wedding had been only a few weeks ago, but it hadn't taken him long to feel as if he'd known Lily forever. Their connection baffled him, because two people couldn't be more different from each other than they were. But they worked somehow, and he was smart enough not to question it.

Eventually she smiled, and he felt as if he'd scored a touchdown. "Okay. But if I think I'm getting in the way, I'll make my excuses and leave. Agreed?"

"Whatever you say."

On impulse, he offered her his hand, and he was thrilled when she took it without hesitation. Strolling across the street hand in hand with Lily should have felt strange, but he was astonished to find it felt as natural as anything he'd ever done in his life.

Pausing near the wrecked pirate ship that was part of the town's huge redwood play structure, Mike found his adventurous daughter at the wheel, calling out instructions to the boy she considered her cousin.

"Here they come, Parker!" she shouted, pointing to an imaginary ship in the distance. "They look mean."

"Not to worry, Cap'n. We're way tougher than them." Manning the water cannon, he fired at their invisible enemies and announced, "Bull's-eye!"

After the young swashbucklers had celebrated their victory, Mike strode to the base of the ladder and called out, "Permission to come aboard?"

"Oh, hi, Daddy," she greeted him, all trace

of her earlier intensity gone in a delighted grin. "Did you see us?"

"Yeah, you both did great. Can I take you away from your crew and talk to you for a second?"

He'd meant to keep his tone light, but she was a sharp kid, and her happy expression instantly clouded over. "Is something wrong?"

"Just something I wanna run by you is all."

"Okay." She glanced over and saw Lily at the edge of the playground, and her bright expression righted itself. Waving excitedly, she hollered, "Hi, Lily! Did you see us?"

"Yes, I did. You've got a nice hand on the tiller, Cap'n." Abby gave her a puzzled look, and Lily laughed. "It means you're a top-notch sailor."

"Oh. Thank you."

Athletic as any boy in town, she clambered down the ladder and followed Mike and Lily from the playground. He knew he was only delaying the inevitable, but he took his time leading them to a bench under the shade of one of the enormous oaks that had given his hometown its name.

When the three of them were seated, he took a deep breath and got right down to it. "Your mom was at the kindergarten graduation today, Abs. She wants to meet you."

"Why?"

The question caught him off guard, and he searched for a way to answer it. Since he'd flatly refused to speak to his ex-wife, he really had no idea what was driving her sudden bout of maternal concern. "Well, it's been a while and I'm guessing she missed you."

"Why?" Abby repeated, her face wrinkling into a baffled frown. "She doesn't even know me."

Completely out of his emotional depth, Mike flashed Lily a "save me" look. That got him a reassuring smile, and she offered another one to Abby. "I think that's the whole idea, sweetie. I talked to her for a while, and she said she regrets missing so much time with you."

"So she thinks leaving was a mistake?"

"That's the impression I got." Shifting one of Abby's braids back over her shoulder, Lily said, "It seems to me that she wants to mend fences with you. Or at least try."

Abby's eyes flicked to him. "What about Daddy?"

A sharp retort threatened to spoil the whole forgiveness vibe Lily was trying to create, and Mike choked it down out of respect for his daughter's feelings. "This isn't about me. It's about you. And your mom," he added through gritted teeth.

It was killing him to crack open the most painful part of his past again, but Lily was right. The choice of whether or not to meet Dana should be Abby's, not his.

"Will you be there?" she asked, giving him the kind of trusting look that would make him walk through fire to save her.

"Aren't I always?" She nodded, and he gathered her in for a hug. Planting a kiss on top of her head, he murmured, "Love you, Abs."

Sighing, she wrapped her arms around him and held on tight. "Love you, too, Daddy."

He would do anything for his little girl, he acknowledged with a sigh of his own. Even if it meant wrangling with a woman who made him want to chew iron and spit out nails.

"I think this calls for a celebration," Lily announced brightly. "Who wants ice-cream wheels?"

"Me!" Abby shouted, hand in the air. "I like vanilla, and my crew likes chocolate."

"One of each, coming up. I'll meet you at yonder island with your provisions, Cap'n." She pointed toward a picnic table at the edge of the play area, and Abby saluted before bounding away to rejoin Parker on the ship.

"You're really good at that pretending stuff," Mike complimented her.

"Playtime is a wonderful opportunity for

broadening your perspective, no matter how old you are."

He laughed. "Is there a message in there for me somewhere?"

"Only if you hear one."

With that, she stood and headed toward the café where he'd found her. She moved at a leisurely pace, and this time he was confident she was sending him a message. Follow or not, it's up to you.

Up to now, all his experience had been with women who ended up demanding more than he cared to give them. Young and overwhelmed by the rocky road she'd taken in life, Dana had needed him to stand between her and the world, shielding her from her own mistakes.

Lily, on the other hand, stood beside him as a partner, working with him to create a successful business out of nothing. Full of kindness, she wasn't averse to giving him a kick when he needed one, and she'd forged a strong, loving bond with Abby that he still had a hard time believing. Then there was her willingness to wade into the complicated mess Dana had made and try to improve the situation. Simply because she believed it was the right thing to do.

What kind of person did that? he wondered as he watched her stroll away. Then he realized that standing there trying to answer that question on his own would get him nowhere. For the first time in years, he'd met a woman who fascinated him enough that he was tempted to put aside his misgivings and take a shot at figuring out what made her tick.

Before he had a chance to do something stupid like talk himself out of it, he hurried forward and quickly fell in step beside her. She didn't say anything when he took her hand again, but she flashed a brilliant smile up at him, and his foolish heart rolled over in his chest.

And despite his vow to keep his distance from her, he found himself grinning back.

Chapter Nine

Sunday morning, Mike was sitting alone at the kitchen table when his mother came downstairs. Dressed in her nicest clothes for church, she pulled up short when she saw him. "Is something wrong?"

"No," he answered evenly, sipping his coffee. "Why?"

"Usually you're still out in one of the barns this time on a Sunday."

He met her worried look with what he hoped was a calm expression. Lily's comments about him finding a way to forgive Dana had gotten him thinking about a lot of other things he'd been ignoring. They'd been piling up over the past few years because he wasn't keen to face up to them. He'd kept telling himself it was because he was so busy with the family businesses and raising Abby, but sometime during his restless night, he'd finally admitted that wasn't the real reason that he'd been neglecting them.

Once he'd embraced that epiphany, a long-overdue bout of soul-searching led him to see that his lapsed faith was one of the parts of his life that used to be good and had turned sour. At the top of the list, actually. The problem was, he was reluctant to make too big a deal out of it with anyone else. There was a good chance that this experiment would end up being a complete disaster for him, and if he wanted to repair his relationship with God, he'd have to dust himself off and start over again.

It didn't escape him that he wasn't even considering retreating from his faith altogether the way he had before. He blamed Lily. His well-intentioned but pesky business partner had been a better influence on him than he could have ever anticipated.

Hoping he sounded casual about the idea, he said, "I thought I might go to Pastor Wheaton's service with you and Abby this morning."

Worry quickly gave way to delight, and she wrapped her arms around his shoulders from behind. "Praise be, Michael. It's been so long, I was beginning to wonder if you'd ever set foot in a church again."

"Well, I'd have to if I'm gonna give Abby away at her wedding someday, wouldn't I?" he teased to lighten up her intense mood. He didn't want to get her hopes up and then change his mind later on. "I figured it'd be better not to wait till then, though."

"I agree with you a hundred percent on that one," she assured him as she turned on the oven. After pulling one of her delicious egg and sausage casseroles from the fridge, she slid it into the oven to warm up and set the timer. Then she turned to him with one of those smug Mom looks he and his siblings still despised even though they were all grown up now. "I'm assuming we have Lily to thank for opening your eyes."

"Possibly." Smothering a grin, he lifted his Best Dad Ever mug for a sip and pretended the accounts printout in front of him was the most fascinating thing he'd ever read.

"Possibly," she mimicked, smacking him across the shoulders with an oven mitt. "My word, you're the most aggravating child any mother has ever been cursed with."

Aimed at all of them at some point in time, the insult had been heard so often around the old farmhouse, it had become a running family joke. Chuckling, he came back with the usual response. "Yeah, but I'm still your favorite."

"That y'are," she confirmed, beaming proudly at him. Her eyes drifted to the gallery of frames on the wall, growing misty as they settled back on him. "At the risk of sounding like a sappy old woman, I have to say you remind me more of your father every day."

Unexpected, her praise brought a lump into his throat. Swallowing hard, he managed to say, "Thanks. That means a lot to me."

"I know." Sitting next to him, she covered his hand with hers. Small but strong, that hand had done more work than most people would believe it was capable of. Her hazel eyes bored into his, and he fought the urge to squirm the way he had when he was a child and she had something important to tell him.

"I never thanked you for coming home to take over when your father died, Michael. This place is huge and difficult to run, with the crops and all the animals we've always had here. And when the racing business went away—" Pausing, she shook her head. "It would've broken my heart, but if you hadn't taken over, we'd have had no choice other than to sell the farm."

Uncomfortable with her glowing assessment of him, he shifted in his seat. Tapping into the optimism he'd been learning from Lily, he teased, "Aw, you're a hardheaded O'Connell. You'd have figured something out."

"I was so lost without him, and trying to keep the business going was more than I could manage on top of that. Then you and Abby came, and I had something more important to do than grieve. The two of you were a gift straight from God Himself."

Not long ago, that kind of comment would have irked him, at best. At worst, he'd have gotten to his feet and left the room to avoid insulting his mother's beliefs. But with Lily's patient, persistent nudging, he'd started on the road to forgiving past wrongs and getting on with his life. Spending one morning in church wasn't the solution, he knew.

But it was a start.

Smiling at the generous, determined woman who'd raised him, he said, "Abby loves being here on the farm. We both do."

"When you first got here, I wasn't sure you'd ever feel that way."

"I didn't much like giving up the independence I had at the ranch. But I gotta admit the food here's a lot better."

"Well, thank you."

She added a smile as the oven timer started dinging. The stove was a relic from long before he was born, and lately the sound it made had a tired wheeze and skipped a couple of beats between each chime. This Christmas, the family should chip in on one of those stainless-steel gourmet ovens for her. She'd love it, and they'd all get to enjoy the recipes she was bound to try with her fancy new toy. It was a win-win.

Abby came bouncing down the stairs, stopping abruptly when she saw what he was wearing. She was used to seeing him in jeans and T-shirts, so his buttoned-down appearance must have been quite a shock. "Where are you going, Daddy?"

"To church with you and Grammy."

"Really?" When he nodded, she gave him a sober look. "Does that mean you're not mad at God anymore?"

"I'm working on it," he replied truthfully. Then, since he was being so honest, he added, "Lily got me started, so we'll see how it goes."

"If you get stuck, she can help you," she suggested brightly. "She's a real good teacher."

Despite the serious nature of their conversation, Mike felt a smile taking over his face. That happened a lot when he thought about Lily, he realized. He was well and truly snared, but for some strange reason he didn't care. "Yeah, she is. Anyone who can train Charlie not to jump up on the kitchen table is a pro in my book."

The three of them chatted while they ate, making quick work of Mom's breakfast. During the drive into town, Mike noticed he had a death grip on the steering wheel and made a conscious effort to relax. He hadn't been anywhere near a church since his father's funeral three years ago, and while he knew returning was the right thing to do, he wasn't looking forward to taking that first step.

As he pulled in and parked, it struck him that the Shepherd's Chapel was just the way he remembered it from his childhood. Same simple white building, same tall glass windows sparkling in the morning sunlight. His feet began dragging as he approached the steps, but he forced himself to keep going out of pure Irish pride. He didn't want anyone to know just how hard it was for him to come back after being away for so long.

Inside, he paused in the doorway to take stock of his surroundings before plunging in. People he'd known all his life sat in the pews, laughing and chatting with their neighbors before the service. Following Mom and Abby to where the rest of the family was sitting, he took in the bright, welcoming feel of the little church where he'd learned the hymns Dad used to sing while they did their morning chores.

Standing back to let the ladies walk down

the row of seats ahead of him, he felt a touch on his shoulder, as if a strong hand had settled there for a moment before letting go. A warm sensation washed over him, and he couldn't help thinking his father was reaching down from heaven to let Mike know he was glad to see him there.

As if that wasn't enough, Lily glanced up from her conversation with Erin, her gorgeous blue eyes lighting up in delight when they landed on him. Mike's heart rolled over like a love-starved hound, and he tried to look cool as he slid into the open spot on the end of the pew. He hadn't quite recovered from her silent greeting when she nearly knocked him on the floor with one of her dazzling smiles.

She leaned across Abby to murmur, "You're just full of surprises, aren't you?"

"I guess. Judging by all these folks trying to look like they're not staring at me, you're not the only one who's shocked to see me."

"Not shocked. Happy." Putting an arm around Abby, Lily gave her a quick hug. "You must be, too."

"Daddy's almost not mad at God anymore," his daughter chirped. "He said you helped him."

Lily gave him a long, thoughtful look. "Did he?"

Thankfully, Pastor Wheaton walked through

a side door and over to the lectern to lead the congregation in the first hymn. When they'd finished, Abby climbed into Mike's lap, and they listened to a sermon about the love of a father for his children and how it could change the world.

But for Mike, the words faded into the background when Abby yawned and rested her head on his shoulder. The light sweater she was wearing slipped down her arm, and Lily reached over to tug it back into place. The motherly gesture did something to his heart, and for the first time Mike didn't bother hiding what he was feeling when their eyes met over Abby's sleepy head.

To his astonishment, he saw those same emotions swirling through those forget-me-not eyes. For so long, he'd wondered if he'd ever meet a woman brave and generous enough to take on not only him but his daughter, too.

Finding her sitting beside him in this simple white church was almost more than he could have dared to hope for. But as they sat there in a family circle of their own, the hopeful part of him that still existed started to believe.

After church, Maggie invited Lily to what she blithely called "lunch." The casual way she did it left Lily expecting an everyday family gathering as they'd done the day she found Charlie under Bea's mulberry bush.

This time, the meal ended up being an all-out barbecue, including several large picnic tables filled with Kinley relatives and friends from all over the county.

"What's the occasion?" she asked Mike, who was turning delicious-smelling ribs and ears of corn on a huge grill, while she helped set places for everyone.

He gave her the kind of blank look her students had reserved for forgotten homework and shrugged. "Yesterday, Mom said she felt like having a get-together. We used to do this kinda thing a lot, so I guess she's been missing it."

Lily clearly heard what he wasn't saying: that the big picnics had ended when Justin died. She'd become very fond of Maggie over the summer, and it was good to know she was finally beginning to recover from his loss. *Small steps,* Lily thought with a smile. Like her son.

Who was currently eyeing her with a suspicious male expression. "What's going on in that head of yours?"

"Just thinking how comforting it is to know that no matter how bleak things may seem, we all come to terms with things in our own time. And how nice it is when they work out for the best."

"I'm not even gonna pretend to follow that." With a practiced motion, he flipped over a rack of ribs, and the flames sizzled with the fresh sauce he poured over top of the browning meat.

Looking around the festive gathering, Lily took in the brilliant, sunny afternoon that was a pleasant start to a busy week to come. It was a hot day in mid-July, but a capricious breeze swept over the rolling hills and through the side yard to keep everyone cool. A spirited game of horseshoes was going on in the pit Mike's youngest brother, Josh, had put in out back, and children of various ages were running in circles around the water toy Erin had hooked up for them. At random intervals, the plastic flower on the end whipped around and doused them, making them squeal and laugh.

Not to be left out, Charlie kept jumping into the spritzing water, barking as he tried to catch it in his mouth. A small shape emerged from the shadows beneath a nearby tree, and Lily saw Sarge edging closer to see what all the fuss was about. When Charlie inadvertently splashed him, the older dog withdrew a few steps but didn't abandon the fun altogether. Instead, he sat just outside the splash zone, ears perked with an interest in his surroundings that he didn't normally show.

Apparently, even the timid terrier was feeling more upbeat these days, she mused with a little smile. It was wonderful to see.

"So," Mike commented, still focused on the grill, "I called Dana this morning. She and I are meeting for lunch at the Oaks Café tomorrow. I figured if we met out in public, it'd go better."

"For you or for her?"

"Both of us, I guess," he confided in a grudging tone. "I'm not exactly thrilled with the whole thing, but since it's what Abby wants, I'll just have to make it work."

Lily was overjoyed with the news, and her instinct was to hug him and gush about how proud she was of him for having the courage to face down his past troubles this way. But his offhand way of sharing his plan warned her that he wouldn't take that kind of reaction well, so she settled for patting his arm. "Good for you, Mike. I hope it goes well."

In her memory, she replayed her first conversation with Dana at Abby's graduation. She'd been astonished when the woman sounded so confident that despite his obvious bitterness toward her, Mike would eventually come around and do what was fair. Now, though, she understood Dana's faith in him. And was pleased to find she shared it without hesitation.

Mike was far from perfect, but he was a good guy. In her estimation, acknowledging and overcoming his flaws made him a much better person than if he pretended not to have any at all.

"Aw, come on," he chided with a knowing look. "Don't I get a hug or something?"

"I wasn't sure you wanted one, here in front of so many people."

Turning, he gazed down at her with genuine affection warming his eyes. "From you, I'd take one anytime."

She was only too happy to oblige him, and as he held her close, he murmured, "Thank you, Lily."

Pulling back, she noticed he didn't seem ready to let go of her, which suited her just fine. Standing there circled in those strong arms, she smiled up at him. "For what?"

"Everything. I don't think you realize how much you've done for Abby and the rest of the family since you got here. Especially me," he added in an uncharacteristic show of emotion.

Delighted by the revelation, she felt her pulse zoom up several notches, and it took everything she had to keep her voice steady. "I'm glad to hear that, because you've all done a lot for me, too. Especially you."

"Crazy, huh?" Chuckling, he shook his head. "We're like night and day."

"It takes both those things to keep life on Earth moving along on an even keel."

"Well, you're the teacher," he drawled with the lopsided grin she'd come to adore. "I guess you must be right."

After enduring so many years of derision from people who didn't understand her commitment to teaching, it was wonderful to find someone who not only approved but valued her accomplishments. When Mike looked at her, he saw so much more than what was visible on the surface. He'd been the first man to do that with her, and she'd always be grateful to him for that.

"Just remember that next time we're arguing," she teased.

The grin widened, and his eyes twinkled with the humor she'd seen a lot more of lately. "Yes, ma'am."

Chapter Ten

Lily paused outside the school district office, trying to shake off the feeling that she had no business being here. She didn't have an appointment, but she definitely had an agenda, and she was counting on the good reputation she'd built for herself while filling in for Mrs. Howard to get her in the door. While she composed herself, it struck her that the building was practically empty and silent as a tomb compared with the constant buzz of activity that occupied it during the school year.

Quit stalling, she scolded herself sternly. Pulling herself up to the formal bearing she'd learned for her debutante ceremony, she reached out and resolutely turned the knob that led into the outer office. She figured this might well be her only chance to snare a teaching position in the town she'd come to think of as home. Being timid wasn't going to get her anywhere.

"Good morning, Mrs. Nelson," she greeted the lone occupant with a smile. "How's your summer going so far?"

"Very well," the plump middle-aged woman responded in kind. "I hear you've been busy yourself. My granddaughter Kennedy is one of your riding students, and she can't stop talking about the horse show. We can't thank you enough for giving her such a fun summer at the farm."

"I'm so glad to hear that. She's done a fabulous job with her lessons, and all the ponies love the apples she brings them."

They chatted back and forth about children and how quickly they grow up, until the motherly woman gave Lily a knowing look. "Since you're all dressed up, I'd imagine you're here to see Mr. Allen."

"Yes." She almost added "only if he has time," but managed to stop herself before she backpedaled right out the door. Instead, she tightened her grip on the handle of her briefcase and waited while Mrs. Nelson called into the principal's private office on the intercom.

"Go right in, dear." She pointed down a short hallway and added, "I'll say a little prayer."

The kind offer eased some of her nerves, and Lily smiled back at her. "I'll take it."

Mr. Allen's door was open, and strains of a Mozart piano concerto drifted out into the corridor. When she knocked, he stood and greeted her with a warm handshake. "It's wonderful to see you, Miss St. George. I hope you're enjoying the lovely weather we've been having."

"Very much, thank you." He motioned for her to sit, and she gratefully sank into a chair opposite his desk. He had to know why she was here, she thought as he sat down and folded his hands on his leather blotter. But should she launch into her spiel, or let him start the conversation?

To her great relief, he gave her the same look his receptionist had earlier. "Can I assume you're here about a job?"

"Yes, sir." Even to her own ears, that sounded meek, and she tapped into some of the moxie she'd inherited from her free-spirited mother. "As you know, my peer reviews from the teachers were outstanding for the short time I was in charge of Mrs. Howard's class. The environment here at Oaks Crossing Elementary, with its small classes and dedicated staff, would be ideal for any teacher. I'd very much like to continue making a contribution here."

Her heart was pounding so hard, she was nearly out of breath by the time she reached the end of her pitch. Fortunately, she'd practiced it so many times, it had ended up sounding as confident as humanly possible when her pulse was racing along like a hummingbird's. Hyperventilating during an interview wouldn't go over well, so she forced herself to breathe slowly. Not only did it settle her nerves, it gave her something to focus on besides how long it was taking him to respond to her proposal.

"I'll be honest with you," he began in an apologetic tone that didn't bode well. "We don't currently have any positions open anywhere in the district. Most of our teachers are parents of children attending school here, and they're committed to staying for many years to come."

He paused, and she realized it was her turn to speak. Hoping to appear professional, she nodded. "I understand."

"That being said, you have exceptional credentials, not to mention a terrific rapport with our students. I'd hate to lose someone of your caliber simply because we refused to think outside the box."

This was her opening, she realized, and she sent up a quick prayer of thanks that he'd offered it to her. "I'm willing to consider any ideas you have."

"I'm not familiar with your financial situation, rent, student loans, that sort of thing. Would you have to work strictly full-time?"

She sensed that he was winging this, and she was more than happy to help him out. "I do have loans, but I rent a studio apartment in town. I'm sure I could make do with whatever salary you have in mind."

He gave her a long look, then rocked back in his chair with a pensive expression. "A few days ago, Mrs. Howard and I were discussing her situation. She wants to continue teaching, but at a reduced level, to give her more time at home with her children. Would you be open to a team classroom scenario with her?"

"Absolutely," Lily blurted, then took a quiet breath so she'd sound more measured. "If she's willing to try it, then I am."

"Let's find out what she thinks." Picking up his phone, he dialed the number from memory and put the call on Speaker. After relaying his idea, he said, "You don't have to answer now, but I thought it was best to get right on this so Miss St. George can make other plans if necessary."

"Not necessary at all," the woman assured him with a light laugh. "I'd love to team teach with you, Lily. You're great with the kids, and I've heard nothing but raves about you from everyone at school. What do you say?"

"It's a deal," she replied, beaming at the man who'd made one of her dreams come true. "Thank you both."

After hanging up, the principal spread his hands in a satisfied gesture. "Well, then, welcome to Oaks Crossing Elementary, Miss St. George. I'll get your paperwork together and call you back next week to make it official. Sound good?"

"It sounds wonderful," she assured him as she stood and shook his hand. "I couldn't ask for more."

"Well, you could have," he corrected her with a chuckle, "but I couldn't have given it to you. This way, we both get some of what we want."

Win-win, Lily thought as she left the office feeling as if she was walking on air. It just didn't get any better than that.

When Dana came through the door of the Oaks Café, every male head in the place turned. And stayed turned, Mike noticed with a wry grin. Whatever her faults might be, there was no denying the woman had the kind of looks that could stop a semi. Too bad they were her best quality.

In his mind, he heard Lily warning him to be nice, and he rose from his seat, waving to get Dana's attention. He'd chosen a table near the window, because he assumed that by now, every busybody in Oaks Crossing knew his ex had blown into town to see him. Rather than hide in a dark corner, he figured it was best to hold this little powwow out in the open where they'd be seen. Tongues were going to wag, anyway, he reasoned. No sense in giving them more to talk about than absolutely necessary.

"Thanks so much for calling," Dana said in a slightly breathless voice. "I wasn't sure you'd be willing to talk to me, much less meet in person."

Recognizing that she was going to push some of his buttons even without meaning to, Mike had rehearsed their reunion while he went about his morning chores on autopilot. He'd considered the possibilities from every angle he could think of, and he was relieved to discover he felt a lot calmer than she looked. "Are you hungry?"

"Maybe after we talk. You start."

Forgive, and you will be forgiven.

The Almighty's advice rang in his mind, and he figured it was best to get that part over with.

Maybe if he led with that, she'd be satisfied and leave them alone. As soon as that thought passed through his mind, he recognized it for the hopeless last-ditch option it was. Hey, a guy could dream.

"Okay. First off, I want you to know I've had a lotta time to think about what happened with us. While I still don't understand why you left, I know you didn't do it to hurt Abby or me."

It took her a few seconds, then her eyes welled with tears. "You mean, you forgive me?"

"Yeah."

"That's just— I don't know what to say," she murmured, taking a napkin from the dispenser to dab at her eyes. Looking over at him, she gave him a shaky smile. "Thank you, Mike. You have no idea how much it means to me to hear you say that, after what I did. You're right that I didn't intend to hurt either of you. I honestly believed you'd both be better off without a mess like me around."

Her voice trembled with genuine anguish, and he realized the girl he'd rescued from the roadhouse was still very much a part of Dana's character. Maybe she always would be. But he'd lost his willingness to carry that anger around with him anymore. Instead, he felt sorry for her and everything she'd lost because she couldn't find a way to leave the past behind her and move on.

The way he needed to do, he realized with a certainty that startled him. Now wasn't the time to examine that too closely, though, so he brought his focus back to why they were here. "That was a long time ago, so we need to let it go. We have something more important to talk about now."

"Abby." When he nodded, Dana gave him a fearful look. "Lily told you what I want?"

"Yeah, but I wanna hear it from you."

After a deep breath, she said, "My mom died earlier this year."

That was the last thing he'd expected to hear, and he frowned in sympathy. "I'm sorry to hear that. Was she sick?"

"Very, so it was actually a blessing when she—" Fresh tears sprung up, and she sipped some water. "Anyway, I was going through the house and found a bunch of photo albums, scrapbooks, stuff like that. One day it hit me that I don't have anything like that for Abby, because I wasn't there when those things happened. That's when I decided that I had to see her."

Sniffling, she got another napkin before fixing him with a desperate look. Mike's first instinct was to protect his daughter, no matter what. But in the face of Dana's wrenching confession, he simply didn't have the heart to play the villain. He didn't used to have a problem with that, and to be honest he wasn't thrilled with the change. Again, he blamed Lily.

"Well, I talked to Abby about it yesterday, and she's okay with meeting you. At the farm, and with me there," he said.

"That's fine. I'm just glad she wants to see me. And that you'll let her," Dana added with sincere gratitude shining in her eyes. "Thank you, Mike."

She reached across the table for his hand, but he pulled it back in a very clear message about where they stood. He might have forgiven her, but he wasn't at the forgetting stage just yet. Truthfully, he wasn't sure he ever would be. Opting not to voice those thoughts, he took two menus from the metal stand and offered her one.

"Water's fine," she said.

Same old Dana, he thought with a grin. If she had more than a few dollars in her wallet, he'd be amazed. "It's on me."

"You don't have to do that."

"I know."

She flashed him the grateful smile he recognized from their first date nearly seven years ago. Except this time, it didn't hit him in the gut the way it had back then. Now it was just a nice smile from a woman he had absolutely no romantic interest in. The difference was striking, and he realized that was his proof that he'd finally gotten past being stomped into the ground and left behind in the dust to raise their daughter on his own.

He had a lot to look forward to these days, he mused as a waitress came to take their lunch order. It was time to quit looking back.

As if on cue, his cell phone started playing the country ringtone he'd assigned to Lily. She'd gone into school to talk about a possible job, and he assumed she was calling for congratulations or sympathy, depending on how it had gone.

"I should take this," he said as he stood. "I'll be right back."

"Take your time. I'm not in a hurry."

Mike went out the door onto the sidewalk for as much privacy as you could get in a place where folks paid attention to everything going on outside their windows. And reported it faithfully to their friends, who passed it along at the first opportunity. "Hey there. How'd it go?"

"I was going to wait and tell you in person, but I'm too excited."

That excitement bubbled across the airy connection, and he knew what she wanted to tell him. But he played dumb to give her the satisfaction of saying it herself. "Yeah? What's up?"

"I got a job offer to team teach kindergarten with Mrs. Howard in the fall. She wants more time at home but doesn't want to stop teaching altogether, so she suggested the two of us could work with the class together. Isn't that amazing?"

"Not a bit. Good teachers are hard to find, and you did a great job for them. They're smart to come up with a way to keep you there. Congratulations, Lily."

"Thanks. I'm pretty psyched."

"I can tell," he replied with a chuckle. "I'd say fantastic news like this calls for a nice dinner. Whattya say?"

"I say I'd love to have dinner with you. It's sweet of you to think of it."

"Yeah, I'm like that now."

"So I've noticed," she said in a ribbing tone. "How's your day going so far?"

"It's been kinda up and down. We got that last round of hay into the barn, but the tractor died partway through, so we had to haul the rest in our pickups. Now I'm at the café with Dana."

"Is that an up or a down?"

He chuckled. "Little of both, as usual. After

we finish eating, she's heading to her hotel and then coming out to the farm."

"Mike, I'm so glad to hear that. Abby must be anxious about meeting her, and it's good not to makc hcr wait any longer than you have to."

Lily's endless concern for his daughter still amazed him. That she could have so much love for someone else's child only highlighted what he valued most about her.

She cared. Deeply and honestly, without reservation or wondering what was in it for her. She was the kind of woman even a jaded guy like him could fall in love with if he wasn't careful.

Shoving the romantic notion aside, he asked, "So, when should I pick you up for dinner?"

"Actually, I'd like to see Dana again, if you don't mind."

Having her there would probably make the whole deal go much easier for him, and he appreciated her suggesting it. "It's fine with me. Thanks for thinking of it."

"I have to go home and change, then I'll meet you at the farm."

"Cool. See you later."

After she'd said goodbye and hung up, he thumbed his phone off and stared at the picture on his home screen for a few seconds. It was of Lily with her arms wrapped around Abby from behind while they were riding double on Gideon. Framed by a clear blue sky and acres of bluegrass, they were laughing at something he'd said just before he snapped the shutter on his camera.

His rodeo girls, he thought, smiling as the background faded to black. They sure were a sweet pair.

Chapter Eleven

Later that afternoon, Abby and Lily were in the kitchen, dishing up kibble for the dogs. With Charlie around, Sarge had taken more of an interest in the family, and he seemed to enjoy having his meals in the house now. It was satisfying to see the old terrier warming up to the people who'd taken him in, and Charlie seemed to enjoy having an older buddy to look up to.

When a snazzy red convertible pulled into the turnaround, one glance out the window showed Lily their visitor was Dana. Stepping from the car, she shook out her blond hair and looked around with a curious expression on her face. Mike had told her his ex-wife had never seen the farm where he'd grown up, and Lily couldn't help wondering what Dana thought of the place.

True to his word, Mike strolled down from the porch and greeted her politely, hands stuck in the front pockets of his jeans. It was a seemingly casual pose Lily had come to understand meant he wasn't thrilled with what he was facing but would clench his fists and tough it out because that's what he had to do.

Apparently, Abby picked up on the gesture, too, because she cast a worried look up at Lily. "Daddy doesn't want to do this, does he?"

"He wants what's best for you," Lily said as diplomatically as she could manage. Reaching out, she flipped the girl's sun-streaked French braid back over her shoulder. "Since you want to meet your mom, he'll go along to make you happy."

"That's what he said, too," she whispered in a miserable tone. But she was staring at their guest, clearly fascinated by the stranger who was her long-absent mother. "She's beautiful, isn't she?"

"Very. You look just like her."

Swiveling to Lily, those china-blue eyes rounded with astonishment. "Do you really think so?"

"Yes, I do." Sensing a little levity would help defuse the girl's conflicting feelings, she forced a lighthearted giggle. "In about ten years, your daddy's going to have his hands full keeping the boys in line."

"I'll take care of them myself," Abby insisted with a confidence Lily wished she'd had at that age. It had taken her a long time to figure out what kind of life she wanted, much less come up with a way to make it happen.

"I don't doubt that a bit. Are you ready to go meet your mom?"

To her surprise, Abby slipped her small hand into Lily's, casting a pleading look up at her. "Will you come with me?"

She was touched by the girl's faith in her, but Lily hesitated. "This is family business. Maybe I should wait in here."

"You're family," Abby informed her matter-of-factly. "Besides, if you're there, Daddy will feel better. He's always happier when you're around."

The unexpected revelation made what had been a fabulous day even better, and Lily relented with a smile. "Whatever you want, sweetie."

Hand in hand, they walked onto the front porch, where Dana was sitting on the swing, sipping lemonade from a tall glass. Mike stood with his back to the railing, arms crossed and jaw set with determination to somehow make it through what must be a terribly awkward situation for both of them. Lily couldn't hear what they were saying, but their voices were calm enough, and to her it seemed that they were trading small talk like civilized people. Apparently, breaking the ice with lunch had been a good idea.

When she and Abby appeared at the end of the porch, Dana's eyes flicked to her daughter and settled there with a wistfulness that tugged at Lily's soft heart. Standing, the slender woman glanced at Mike, who answered her unspoken question with a single nod. He kept his cool, though, staying where he was and allowing her to meet Abby on her own.

"Hello, Abby." Clearly terrified that she might be rejected, Dana offered a faint smile. "It's been a long time since we last saw each other, so you probably don't remember me. I'm your mother."

Abby gave the woman a thoughtful once-over and met her gaze as directly as any adult could have managed under the same circumstances. "I know. Lily says I look like you."

That comment hung in the air like a bomb waiting to go off, and Lily debated whether or not to step in and smooth the road a little. Finally, she offered her hand. "It's nice to see you again, Dana. Did you have any trouble getting here?"

"My rental car has a GPS system, so I was fine. I have something for you, Abby," she added as if she'd just recalled that. She took a festively wrapped box from the wicker table and handed it to her daughter. "It's something I would've liked when I was a young lady like you. I hope you like it."

Abby flashed Mike a questioning look, and his jaw relaxed just enough for him to give her an encouraging smile. "It's okay, Abs. It's from your mom, so you can open it."

While the girl tore into her present, Dana caught Mike's eye and mouthed, "Thank you." His expression softened ever so slightly, and he nodded again. Seeing his bitterness ebb even that tiny amount was like watching an iceberg begin to thaw, and Lily fought down the impulse to reward him with a hug. She knew it wasn't easy for him to trust his ex-wife this way, and Lily recognized it was a huge step forward for this stubborn, protective man who'd captivated her from the first time she laid eyes on him.

Putting that thought aside, she dragged her mind back to the front porch and Abby's gift. Inside the wrapping was a white jewelry box with running horses painted around the sides and a lovely horse head on the lid.

"Open it," Dana urged. When Abby obliged,

the music box began playing a gentle, soothing tune. "It's a Native American lullaby a friend of ours in New Mexico wrote for you when you were born. I used to sing it to you when you were a baby."

After listening for a few moments, Abby closed the lid but kept the box cradled in her hands. Glancing over at Mike, she asked, "Did your friend really write that song for me?"

"Yes, he did. He was older than me, so he kind of thought of you like the granddaughter he never had."

Reassured, she met Dana's anxious gaze with a direct one of her own. It wasn't exactly a trusting look, Lily noticed, but it was much less skeptical than it had been a few minutes ago. "It's very pretty. Thank you."

"You're welcome. Your dad said you've got a new puppy. Do you think I could meet him?"

"His name is Charlie. He just ate, so he's in the barn with Sarge."

"That's okay," Dana replied eagerly. "I like barns."

The poor woman was so on edge, Lily suspected she'd do absolutely anything Abby wanted her to do. That she'd had a gift specially made for her daughter said something about the lengths Dana was willing to go to reconcile with Abby, and Lily silently urged the girl to give her mother a chance.

Setting the jewelry box on the table, Abby gazed up at Dana as if she was trying to make up her mind. Finally, she said, "He still jumps on people sometimes."

"No problem. I'm sturdier than I look."

Now that she'd made something akin to progress, some of the tension left Dana's face. The rest of it fell away when Abby took her hand and led her down the steps toward the barn. Watching them go, Lily realized she'd been holding her breath. She let it out in a relieved rush and turned to Mike. "I think that went well."

"Yeah." Sinking into a wicker chair, he crossed a boot over the knee of his threadbare jeans and sighed. "I guess Dana showing up here was for the best."

"Best for Abby, or for you?" Sitting in the chair beside his, Lily poured them each a glass of lemonade. After handing Mike his drink, she curled up in the generous seat and took a sip.

He gave her a long look that told her nothing about what was going on behind those impossibly blue eyes. If he hadn't looked so much like a windblown surfer, she'd have described him as dark and mysterious. It wasn't the only contradiction she'd noticed in this strong, stubborn man, but it was definitely one of the most intriguing.

"I'm not following you," he finally said.

"Carrying a grudge takes a lot out of a person. It's energy they could use for more productive things."

"Such as?"

"Love," she blurted without thinking. The corners of his eyes crinkled just a tad, but he didn't tease her for having her head in the clouds, as she'd expected. Taking that as a prompt to continue, she went on. "Letting go of bitter memories leaves us open for new things that are much more important."

"Forgive, and you will be forgiven."

Totally stunned to hear this formerly lost sheep quoting the Bible, Lily stammered, "Yes, I suppose so."

"One of Dad's favorite sayings," Mike confided with a smile. "I guess I was so angry over what's gone on these past few years, I forgot how important that is." Reaching over, he took Lily's hand and wrapped it in his much larger one. "But now I remember, thanks to you."

"I— Well— Um—" Realizing she sounded like a complete idiot, Lily swallowed some lemonade to buy time for her to regain her composure. The warmth of Mike's fingers on hers made it almost impossible for her to think, but the last thing she wanted was for him to let her go. Ever.

Flashing her one of those cocky grins, he chuckled. "Y'know, for a college girl you're pretty easy to rattle."

"I had a sheltered upbringing," she confessed shyly.

"Yeah, I figured. It's kinda nice to find a woman who's not obsessed with her job or jaded from being kicked around by her ex."

"I'm glad you feel that way, since I can't change it."

"That's good to hear, 'cause you're perfect just the way you are."

Leaning in to bridge the gap between them, he brushed a gentle kiss over her lips. She got the impression that he was asking her a question, and she sighed in response. She felt him smile, then he reached out a calloused hand to cradle her cheek and draw her in for another, much longer kiss.

When he pulled away, she summoned a smile for him. He deserved to know the truth about her, but the selfish part of her wanted to keep this perfect moment just as it was, unspoiled by reality. She understood that loyalty meant everything to Mike, a trait reinforced by his long-term bitterness over Dana's betrayal. When Mike found out who Lily really was, she feared the memory of this very special afternoon would be all she'd have left of what might have been.

But as wrong as it had been to deceive him, it was worse to continue the charade. Judging by her reaction to his touch, their relationship was rapidly sliding past the friendship stage and into something that was exhilarating and terrifying at the same time. He had a right to know the truth about her before things between them went any further.

Then, out of nowhere, a long black limousine appeared at the end of the driveway and slowly made its way toward the parking area near the house. The license plate read LSG1, and she barely held back a gasp when her terrified heart launched itself into her throat.

"He must be lost," Mike said with a chuckle, pushing up from the arms of his chair. "I'll see if I can get him straightened out."

Reaching out, Lily stopped him with a hand on his arm. He gave her a questioning look, then seemed to pick up on her reaction to their visitor and frowned. "What is it?"

"He isn't lost," she explained simply. "He's here for me."

Mike's eyes flicked to the car, then settled

back on her like a lead weight. In them she saw a swirling mix of emotions, none of them good. He didn't say anything, and as the silence stretched between them, she felt the distance growing with each nervous heartbeat.

"This isn't how I wanted to tell you." Hearing the tremor in her voice, she paused to steady her nerves as she stood up. "The car belongs to my grandfather Leland St. George. He owns—"

"Half the state," Mike finished for her. The brusque attitude he'd had when she first met him had returned full force. As if that wasn't bad enough, he eyed her with open disdain. "So, what're you doing out here in the sticks, slumming with us common folk?"

The insult struck her like a physical blow, but she refused to knuckle under to it. Instead, she raised herself up to her full height and glared back at him. "It's not like that. *I'm* not like that, and you know it."

"I'm not sure what I know," he retorted in a terrifyingly calm voice. "Have a nice trip back to Louisville, Your Highness."

Turning on the heel of his boot, he stalked down the steps and away from the house. Avoiding the turnaround, he headed for one of the barns. He flung open the sliding door and slammed it behind him with a finality that sent Lily's heart plunging to her feet.

Unfortunately, her own misery had to wait. Only a family emergency would bring her other world crashing into this one, and she hurried over to the driver waiting patiently beside the car.

"Hello, Miss Lily," Vernon said, bowing slightly. "I'm sorry to interrupt you so abruptly, but I wasn't able to reach you by phone. When I went by the address your grandmother gave me, your landlady told me I'd find you here."

"I turned my cell off earlier, so that's my fault. Something must be wrong, or you wouldn't be here."

"Your grandfather had a stroke this morning. He's in the hospital and was asking for you, so your grandmother sent me to fetch you."

To say goodbye, Lily filled in the blank for him. The thought of her kindhearted grandfather being frightened enough to send for her made her sick inside. Tears blurred her vision, and it was all she could do to nod. He gave her a sympathetic look, then stepped away to open the rear door for her.

After he'd settled into his seat, he glanced into the rearview. "Would you like to stop to pick up some clothes?"

"I'm fine, Vernon. Just get me to Grandpa as fast as you can."

Before it's too late.

He should've known better.

That self-condemning phrase repeated over and over in his head, in rhythm with the curry brush he was using to clean up Gideon's mud-caked coat. It hadn't rained in a week, so where the gelding had picked up so much dirt was beyond him. The fact that his partner in crime, Chance, was spotless only made it more of a mystery.

Mindless tasks like this one usually helped him think through a problem and come up with a decent solution. This time, though, the problem he was wrestling with had incredible blue eyes and a smile that could brighten the cloudiest day.

And she was a liar.

Just like Dana, that old pessimistic voice in his head chimed in. He hadn't heard it in a while, and he hadn't missed it at all. That it was back now only made him feel more foolish than he already did.

"Of course she's a society girl," he muttered to Gideon while he attacked another clump of mud with the brush. "I should've figured it out sooner. She's smart as a whip and has great taste in everything. Regular folks aren't like that."

"You trying to convince him or yourself?"

Already aggravated, Mike wasn't pleased to find Drew standing outside the stall, peering in at him as if he was on display at a zoo. "Back off, little brother. I'm not in the mood."

"For what? All I know is Lily took off in a limo, and there's a blonde woman playing in the sandbox with Abby."

"That's Dana, here for that visit I told you about," he explained in as patient a voice as he could manage. "I forgot she was even here when I heard what Lily had to say."

"Which was?"

Drew could be a real pain, but the concern in his eyes encouraged Mike to share Lily's stunning revelation.

Letting out a low whistle, Drew said, "I can see how that could upset a guy. Especially one whose ex-wife kicked him on her way out the way Dana did."

Relieved that someone understood, Mike rested his arm on the horse's flank and heaved a long sigh. "You'd think I'd be smarter by now."

"You are." Mike snorted at that, and his brother grinned. "No, really. I mean, a teacher is about as far as you can get from a waitress at a roadhouse."

"Then how is it I still ended up in the same place?"

"From where I'm standing, you didn't. Did you ask Lily why she had to go?"

Mike opened his mouth to respond, then shut it and grimaced. "No. I was so mad about her lying to me, I didn't think to."

"She's been here all summer, and this is the first time anyone from Louisville's come to see her. I'm no expert, but to me that says something's wrong at home. She strikes me as being pretty responsible. Did she call you to say what's going on?"

Mike glanced over to where his cell phone still sat on the hay bale where he'd thrown it in disgust. Beneath the picture of Abby and Lily, a voice mail alert was blinking. He didn't have to be psychic to know it must be a message from Lily.

"I'm the last guy to be telling anyone what to do," Drew said on his way out. "But if it was me, I'd listen to that message before you write the lady off completely."

Since he was walking away, he obviously didn't expect a response, which suited Mike just fine. No matter what Lily had done, in his gut he knew the fair thing was to call and let her explain her reasons for deceiving him. Because angry as he was, he simply couldn't believe she'd purposefully tried to hurt him. Unfortunately, he had another, much more serious problem.

By some manner of ironic insanity, he'd fallen in love with the runaway bridesmaid who'd been lying to him since the first time he laid eyes on her. Judging by the troublesome ache that had settled in his chest, his foolish heart didn't care about any of that. It only wanted Lily back.

What was he supposed to do with that?

Her grandfather looked small.

Lily stood at the foot of his hospital bed, gazing at the man who'd always seemed larger than life to her. Not because of his actual size, but because his personality and his will carried a stature of their own that defied rational explanation. But now, even though he was resting, he no longer looked undefeatable to her.

He looked vulnerable.

"What are you doing here?"

His raspy voice startled her out of her brooding, and she looked up to find those gray eyes were as sharp as ever. She'd actually feared he might not recognize her because of the stroke, and she didn't bother hiding her delight as she slipped into the chair near his bed. "I heard you were lazing around, and I came to give you a kick in the pants."

His chortle lacked its usual power, but she saw the same fondness twinkling in his eyes that she'd enjoyed for as long as she could remember. "Your grandmother likes to fuss, so the doctor's humoring her by keeping me here, that's all."

"Nice try," she chided him, noting the slight drooping on the left side of his craggy face. "How bad was it, really?"

"Bad enough, I suppose. Everyone's tiptoeing around like I'm already set up for my viewing."

Despite the serious situation, Lily couldn't help laughing. "Oh, Grandpa, only you could joke about something like that."

"Tell me about you, Lily. Did you hear about that teaching job you wanted in Oak Ridge?"

"Oaks Crossing," she corrected him gently, smoothing out the wrinkles in the snowy-white sheet that had been expertly folded over the top edge of his light coverlet. Eager to share her good news with him, she forced a smile and continued. "This morning, I accepted an offer to teach kindergarten in the fall."

She went on to tell him the details, then about the riding school and how she planned to introduce her new students to ecology by bringing a baby raccoon from the rescue center into class. She did her best to sound upbeat, but when she was finished, his scowl told her she'd failed miserably.

"And what about the horse trainer you've been gushing about on the phone all summer?"

Although she'd had a firm grip on her emotions until now, the stress of her confrontation with Mike, coupled with her grandfather's condition, finally swamped her. Tears sprang into her eyes, and she furiously blinked them away. "I don't know what to tell you."

"The truth, my darling girl," he said in a soothing tone. Taking her hand, he waited until she met his eyes. "I promise you, no matter what it is, I've heard worse."

Alternately sobbing and sniffling, she poured her heart out to him, not leaving out a single detail of what had gone on since she and Mike met outside Natalie's wedding. When her grandfather gave her a half smile, she asked, "What's so funny?"

"Isn't it obvious?"

"Not really."

"It will be," he said confidently. "You're a smart young woman, and I'm confident you'll figure it out when you see him again."

"I don't think he'll ever want to see me again."

"He will."

"You've never even met him," she pointed out in confusion. "How can you be so sure?"

"Old or young, men are all the same. We bluster and complain, but in the end, all we want is someone to love, who will love us in return. Do you think you could have that with Mike?"

"Maybe," she hedged, "but he's so angry with me, I can't imagine it happening now."

"Give him time to cool off, then explain to him why you kept your background a secret from him."

"That would be wonderful," she admitted, "but I betrayed his trust. I'm not sure he can get over that."

"Anything is possible, Lily," Grandpa murmured as his medication took hold and he drifted off to sleep. "You just need to have a little faith."

Chapter Twelve

The day of the horse show was sunny and warm, one of those gorgeous summer days everyone flooded outside to enjoy. Unfortunately, Mike wasn't in the mood.

Since Lily had dropped her bombshell and been whisked off to Louisville earlier in the week, he hadn't heard a peep from her. Well, that wasn't entirely fair, he corrected himself as he strode into the barn to start prepping the ponies for their big day. She'd called him several times but he'd pressed Ignore and then deleted her voice mails without even listening to them. At first, he hadn't wanted to hear what lame excuse she'd come up with for lying to him for months about who she was.

But as the days had dragged by, he found himself wishing she'd call. That he still had her number on speed dial and knew how to use it was beside the point, he kept telling himself. She was wrong, so she should apologize to him. Petty, maybe, but that was what he'd decided to go with.

On the news, he'd heard about Leland St. George's stroke, and that the family had all gathered around him in a show of love and support for their beloved patriarch. Mike could envision Lily right beside her grandfather, holding his hand, reaching him when no one else could.

The same way she'd done with Mike.

She'd become an integral part of his days, and being without her hurt him so deeply, he felt as if he was just going through the motions. Brooding wasn't getting him anywhere, so he sternly told himself to focus on something else. Mechanically brushing and tacking up half a dozen ponies distracted him for a while. When he was finished, he was grateful when Abby bounced into the stable and climbed onto her perch.

"Hi, Daddy."

"Hey there," he replied with a halfhearted smile. "We're almost ready."

"That's good, because people are starting to show up. Uncle Drew and Aunt Erin helped me decorate the show ring."

Glancing out the side door, he saw the stars-

and-stripes bunting they'd draped along the fence, accented by dark green helium balloons with the Gallimore Riding School logo on them. Seeing them took him back to the day when Lily and Abby had designed the graphic together at the kitchen table while he marveled at how quickly his little girl had become attached to her pretty new teacher.

Suddenly, he missed Lily so much, his chest actually ached. Pushing that aside, he said, "It looks real nice out there, munchkin. Good job."

"Daddy?"

"Yeah?"

"Is Lily's grandpa going to die like Grampa did?"

Once again, Mike was struck by the fact that even though she didn't remember it happening, his father's sudden death had affected Abby greatly. *Like her mother's leaving,* he added silently. All these years, he'd done everything in his power to protect his daughter from the harsh realities of life. And in the end, he'd failed miserably.

"I'm not sure," he answered honestly. "The doctors will do what they can, but then it's up to God."

She absorbed that with a thoughtful expression, then caught him totally by surprise. "It's too bad Lily couldn't be here for the show. When is she coming back?"

Emotion clogged his throat, and Mike cleared it before answering. "I'm not sure she is, Abby. Things are complicated right now."

"Why?"

Good question, he groused. "Because they are."

She cocked her head with the kind of look Mom gave him when she knew something was up. "Did you two have a fight or something?"

"I'm not discussing that with you," he bristled defensively. Normally, that was all someone needed to get the message and back off. But this was his fearless cowgirl, and she shook her head at him with a sigh.

"That means yes. Whenever I have a fight with Parker or one of my friends, you tell me to step back and look at their side of it. Did you try that?"

She was killing him, turning his own advice against him like this. But he could hardly blame her. She was six years old, and to her the world was black-and-white. Someday, when she was older, she'd learn how gray things could get. But he didn't want this to be that day.

"I think we need to get these horses lined up for the opening parade," he suggested, hoping that would end the interrogation for now. "Wanna give me a hand?"

She gave him a long, pitying look but jumped down and took Sparkle's lead rope from him. After handing off another, he grabbed the last four himself and followed Abby and her ponies out into the ring.

Standing at the rail facing a crowd of beaming moms and dads, he was completely out of his element. Copying what he'd seen Lily do, he held out his arms in the quieting gesture she used. When everyone had settled, he dredged up a friendly smile.

"Hello, everyone, and welcome to the First Annual Gallimore Riding School Show. The kids have worked real hard on their skills, from barn work to tacking up to actually riding. They've done a great job, and I think we should give them a big round of applause."

They all obliged, and not only did it please the kids immensely, it gave him a chance to get his bearings. Strolling out to the center, he called out, "Riders, mount up!"

A buzz of anticipation went through the crowd, echoed by the first six kids waiting in the "riders only" section of the stands Drew had built for the occasion. Erin helped each one mount, sending them off with an encouraging smile and a pat on the shoulder. Dressed in her favorite cowgirl outfit, Abby hung on the far rail, braids bobbing as she cheered her friends through the simple patterns they'd been learning for the past month.

In all honesty, Mike was a little stunned at how well everything went. No one fell off or went the wrong way, although that probably had as much to do with the steady, reliable ponies than any particular riding skill. But in the end, when all the kids gathered in the middle of the paddock to take their bows, he had to admit that their first show was a remarkable success.

When Abby came over to stand beside him, he swept her into his arms with a grin. "Well, Abs, what did you think of your very first horse show?"

"It was awesome, Daddy," she replied in her usual bubbly way. Then her enthusiasm dimmed a bit, and she said, "I just wish Lily could've been here. It's not the same without her."

Yeah, he thought as he hugged her. *I know what you mean.*

Now that Grandpa was home from the hospital, he seemed to be perking up a little more every day. He grumbled about his physical therapy, scolded his private-duty nurse for harassing him and protested being brought all his meals in bed.

In short, he was getting back to his old self, and Lily was delighted to see it. His eyesight wasn't quite back to normal yet, so she was sitting in a chair by his bed, patiently reading an in-depth article on the current state of affairs in the whiplashing stock market. She didn't understand a word of it, but he followed along well enough, brightening at the good news and glowering at the bad.

The best part of it for her was that he was still here for her to read to. That, and it kept her from wallowing too much in the aftermath of her disastrous decision to lie about who she was to the one person on earth she should have been honest with.

And now it was too late.

Despite her repeated attempts to reach him, Mike had refused to take her calls or make any of his own. That pretty much said it all, she acknowledged with a sigh.

"What is it, Lily?" Grandpa asked, his brow furrowing with concern. "I'm sorry—I didn't think when I asked you to read the paper with me. Is all this dry business news too boring for you?"

"Of course not. Now, where was I?"

Reaching out a shaky hand, he pushed the

paper down so she had to look at him. "Your horse trainer still hasn't called?"

"No." Her chin began trembling, and she got hold of herself before continuing. "I don't think he can forgive me for what I did."

"I wouldn't be so sure about that."

"Why?"

In answer, he nodded at something behind her. When she turned, she saw Mike framed in the open doorway, a solemn look on his face. "I'm sorry to interrupt. Your grandmother said I should come right up."

"That must have given Mrs. Fredericks apoplexy," Grandpa commented with a lopsided grin. "She runs this house with an iron fist. No need to be shy, young man. Come on in."

Edging into the room, Mike asked, "How are you feeling, sir?"

"Better, with my favorite girl here spoiling me. I apologize for taking her away from you so suddenly. I understand you were in the middle of a very serious discussion."

"Well, I—" Mike flashed her a panicked look, as if to ask what she wanted him to say.

"He knows what happened," she explained as calmly as she could. "I told him everything. Including how much I regret keeping something so important from you."

"If you two don't mind, I'm starting to feel drowsy. I think I'll take a little nap."

Lily knew perfectly well the crafty old fox wasn't the least bit tired, but was subtly nudging her out of his room so she could talk to the man who'd driven fifty miles in the middle of a busy week to tell her something. After kissing her grandfather on the forehead, she led Mike down the hall to an empty guest room where they could have some privacy.

She closed the door behind them and stood facing it for a moment, uncertain if she should dread the impending conversation or welcome it. While she tried to pick through her conflicting emotions, Erin's voice echoed in her memory.

Mike's never chased after anyone before. He must think you're something special.

Buoyed by that thought, Lily sent up a quick prayer for patience and turned to face him. The uncertainty shadowing his eyes mirrored her own emotions, and she dredged up a wan smile. "You look the way I feel."

"Back atcha." He didn't sound angry anymore, but the defeated tone in his voice was something new. Folding his arms in that stern posture she'd learned to be cautious of, he went on. "How's your grandfather really doing?"

"He seems all right mentally, but other than

that, I'm not sure yet. This whole thing is like a nightmare."

"I can imagine."

Sympathy shone in his eyes, and a tiny spark of hope flared in Lily's heart. "How was the show?"

"Kids did great, and we got a bunch of new students for the fall. Only one thing went wrong."

That didn't jibe with what he'd said just before that, so she was confused. "What was that?"

"You weren't there."

When he opened his arms for her, she gladly went into them. Cuddled against his chest, wrapped in the warmth of this strong, capable man, she felt as if the knots she'd created for herself just might have a chance at untangling themselves.

Leaning back, she looked up at him somberly. "Mike, I'm so sorry for keeping the truth from you. You have to believe I didn't mean to lie that way."

"Yeah, it took me a while but eventually I figured that out." Giving her the crooked grin she'd come to treasure, he asked, "So why'd you do it?"

"In the past, I had so many people jump to conclusions about me when they found out who my family was. When I went to college, I finally got a fresh start away from Louisville, and it was wonderful to be judged for what I was doing, rather than who my family is. No one expected me to be anything in particular or pretended to like me just so I'd put in a good word for them with my father. It was such a refreshing change."

"Is that why you took a job in a postage-stamp place like Oaks Crossing?"

"Mostly I needed the experience," she replied honestly. "Grandpa gave me a generous check for graduation, so even though I wasn't rich, I had enough for a while. It gave me the freedom to choose what I wanted to do while I hunted for a permanent job."

"Like work at our riding school for peanuts."

"I didn't mind that, since I had a blast working with you and the kids. Besides, it was my idea to take less money to pay for my lessons, remember?"

"Which you've had three of, 'cause we've been so busy with the kids." He grinned down at her with mischief dancing in his eyes. "I'm thinkin' we should do something about that."

"Really?" she replied in mock surprise. "Like what?"

With no warning, he leaned in to kiss her.

Angling a playful look up at him, she asked, "Does this mean you forgive me?"

"Yeah. Seeing as I'm pretty much lost without you these days, I don't really have a choice, do I?"

For all his strength, this was a man with a tender streak that wrapped around the people he cared about in a protective shield Lily had admired from the day he showed up for show-and-tell. Sliding her arms around his waist, she gazed up at him with a reassuring smile. "Now that I'm settled in Oaks Crossing, we should be able to make that work."

"What if you hadn't gotten the kindergarten gig?"

"There are other jobs besides teaching. Assuming you wanted me to be there, I would have figured out a way to stay in town."

"Even before this? I mean, you could go anywhere," he pointed out in a practical tone. "What was keeping you there?"

There were so many ways to answer that question, she realized. But in the end, she let her heart speak for itself. "You and Abby. I can't imagine being anywhere other than where you two are."

Emotions flooded his eyes, and he met her confession with a long, promising kiss. Pulling back just a bit, he rested his forehead on hers with a sigh. "I love you, Lily. I tried not to, but I can't help it."

Offered up in his customarily direct way, the confession made her laugh. "You tried not to?"

"Yeah. It didn't work."

"You don't have to sound so disappointed about it." Framing his face in her hands, she gave him her biggest, best smile. "Seeing as I love you, too."

"You do?" When she nodded, he gave her a sheepish grin. "Well, that's kinda cool."

For all his swagger, there was still a wounded young man inside Mike. Far from discouraging, it only made him more appealing to her. Lily hoped she'd get the chance to bring him out of his shell and watch him enjoy all the things he'd been missing.

"So," he went on in a pensive tone very unlike him, "on the drive here I had a lotta time to think."

That sounded intriguing. "About what?"

"Families. Abby and I have been doing okay on our own, but there's been something missing all this time." Pausing, he dropped a kiss on her lips before adding, "It's you."

Lily's heart bounced up into her throat, and she stared up at him in complete disbelief. "Are you proposing to me?"

"Yeah, I am. Whattya say?"

She didn't even have to think about it. Everything they'd gone through had led them to this point, and while she knew they'd face many more challenges up ahead, she didn't even consider shying away from them.

"I say yes."

Epilogue

"Still hate weddings?" Drew asked while he and Mike struggled with the dress ties they hardly ever wore.

Recognizing that his best man was tossing his own complaint back at him, Mike grinned. "This one's not so bad, I guess."

"You found a woman who loves you and your little girl. You know you're blessed, right?"

Their eyes met in the mirror, and he nodded. "I know."

"Good."

Chuckling, Mike stepped back and brushed some of Charlie's fur off the leg of his trousers. "You sounded like Dad just now."

"That's the nicest thing you've ever said to me," Drew replied without a hint of the sarcasm that normally ran beneath their conversations. "Thanks."

"You're welcome. But don't think I'm gonna be all gooey once I'm married to Lily," he warned with a mock glare. "I'll be leaving that cuddly nonsense up to her and Abby."

Drew laughed, clearly no more worried about that than anything else in his carefree life. "Got it. You ready?"

"Yeah, I am."

"You mean, with fifty people waiting out in the garden, you're not even a little bit nervous?"

"Nope. That's how I know it's right, little brother."

"Meant to be, huh?" Drew asked thoughtfully.

"Something like that. Lily's the one for me, and I'm just glad she feels the same way."

"You make it sound simple."

"It is, when you find the right person. Then you have to work up the guts to take that leap of faith with her."

"I'll have to remember that," Drew commented before shaking off his serious expression with a grin. "Let's go get you two hitched before Lily changes her mind."

"Thanks a lot," Mike grumbled, shoving him

out the door and into the hallway. "Josh didn't have any trouble with the carriage, did he?"

"Nah." Before Mike could ask about the ring, Drew pulled it from his pocket and showed it to him. "We've got it all covered. Just enjoy your wedding. Knowing Lily, it's gonna be your last one."

"Works for me."

Mom had spent every spare moment since their engagement in her garden, pruning and planting so it would look perfect for today. And while Mike wasn't an expert on flowers, in his opinion this patch of the farm rivaled any of the local estates that hosted weddings for the rich and famous.

Pastor Wheaton stood in front of several rows of chairs, at the head of a wide aisle paved with a white runner. Mike and Drew joined him there, and the preacher gave Mike a smiling nod of encouragement. His wife sat at a portable keyboard, as perky as she was in front of the church organ every Sunday. When she started playing an upbeat tune, everyone looked toward the end of the runner.

Abby appeared there, wearing a fluffy pink dress that made her look like one of the sugarplum fairies from her favorite ballet. *His little tomboy,* Mike thought with a muted grin. Someday, he'd be walking her down an aisle somewhere, to become someone's wife. He could only pray she'd find a man who made her as happy as she deserved to be.

Dropping pink rose petals, she smiled at everyone in sight as she all but skipped toward the front. Maid of honor Erin followed behind her, corralling the bouncing flower girl with an arm around her shoulders. Then the wedding march started, and everyone stood expectantly.

There, at the end of that aisle, was the answer to dreams Mike had never dared share with anyone. With her hand tucked beneath her father's arm, Lily moved through the crowd with the dignified grace he'd come to associate with the sweet, headstrong teacher who had dropped into his life and begun mending his battered heart with a smile.

Those poetic words faded away as she joined him, leaving a feeling of gratitude behind. Shaking her father's hand, Mike took Lily's and they faced the pastor the way they'd be doing things for the rest of their lives.

Together.

They traded a long, loving look, and he felt the last bit of his heart fall at Lily's feet. She was marrying him, this woman who'd saved him from himself and shown him what kind of joy he could have if only he opened himself up to it. Nothing said in the short, solemn ceremony came even close to expressing what he was feeling right now, but someday he'd figure out a way to tell her what she meant to him.

For now, he jerked his wandering mind back to the present just in time to take Lily's gold wedding band from Drew.

With his mother's order to speak up ringing in his head, very clearly Mike said, "With this ring, I thee wed."

He slipped the band on her finger, then waited while she repeated the vow and sealed it with his matching ring. Before the preacher could prompt them, Lily flew into Mike's arms for a joyous hug and a long, delighted kiss that earned them a laughing standing ovation from their guests.

"And now it's my pleasure to introduce to you for the first time, Mr. and Mrs. Michael Kinley."

"Michael?" Lily teased.

"Mom insisted. Said she never hears my full name unless she's yelling it at me."

Lily laughed, and Abby popped up between them, eyes shining with excitement. "Can we ride in the carriage now?"

"First, we have to thank our guests," Lily reminded her gently. "Then we can take a little drive and go back to the house for cake."

The three of them made their way down the

aisle of well-wishers to where Josh was waiting in the wedding carriage Mike normally drove. Mike helped them both up, then settled in so Abby was snug between them.

"All set back there?" Josh asked.

"Yeah, but take your time," Mike replied as he loosened the offensive tie and shed his jacket. Leaning his head back, he stared up at the cloudless sky with a sigh. "I could use a nap."

"Daddy!" Abby scolded with a laugh. When he rolled his neck to look over at her, she said, "You're being silly, right?"

"Not really."

"Why are you so tired?" she asked, her face puckering in confusion. "Us girls did all the work."

"Us boys have spent the past two weeks mowing, weeding and mulching so everything would look nice," he reminded her with a chuckle. "On top of everything else we've got going around here, I'm a little tuckered."

"You can rest when the three of us go to Charleston for our honeymoon," Abby informed him sweetly, glancing over her shoulder at his new wife. "Right, Mommy?"

Instantly, Lily's eyes shone bright, and she turned to face Abby more squarely. "You want to call me 'Mommy'?"

"Is it okay? My mom said I should call her 'Dana,' so that way you can be Mommy."

"That was very generous of Dana, and I'll have to thank her next time she visits. It's definitely okay with me." She gathered Abby into a warm hug, then looked over her head at Mike. "If your dad doesn't mind."

For once, he didn't bother thinking something through to be sure it made sense before answering. "Sounds perfect to me."

"We're a family now," Abby announced brightly, wrapping an arm around each of them in a hug. "The way God meant for us to be."

Connecting with Lily's eyes over Abby's head, Mike smiled at his new wife. "My thoughts exactly."

* * * * *

Dear Reader,

Welcome to Oaks Crossing!

When Mike Kinley strolled into my imagination, I was hooked. Who was he? What was his story? And what was making him so grumpy? Basically, the same questions Lily St. George was asking herself when they first met. Through the course of the story, he answered all of them. Stubborn to the core, eventually he was able to let go of the bitterness that had weighed him down, leaving him open to a brighter, more hopeful future. And he was smart enough to recognize it was because of Lily.

Like me, Lily was drawn to the protective single father doing everything in his power to make a good life for his daughter. While she adores children in general, Abby quickly takes over a special place in her heart, which draws her closer to Mike even while she's trying to keep her distance. Throughout the summer, the Kinleys and other residents of Oaks Crossing embrace her and give her a place to belong. That's something we all need, no matter who we are.

If you'd like to stop by for a visit, you'll find me online at miaross.com, Facebook, Twitter and Goodreads. While you're there, send me a message in your favorite format. I'd love to hear from you!

Mia Ross

LARGER-PRINT BOOKS!

GET 2 FREE LARGER-PRINT NOVELS PLUS 2 FREE MYSTERY GIFTS

Love Inspired®

SUSPENSE
RIVETING INSPIRATIONAL ROMANCE

Larger-print novels are now available...

REQUEST YOUR FREE BOOKS!
2 FREE WHOLESOME ROMANCE NOVELS IN LARGER PRINT
PLUS 2 FREE MYSTERY GIFTS

❈❈❈❈❈❈❈❈❈❈❈❈❈❈❈❈❈❈❈❈❈

HEARTWARMING™

❈❈❈❈❈❈❈❈❈❈❈❈❈❈❈❈❈❈❈❈❈

Wholesome, tender romances

YES! Please send me **The Montana Mavericks Collection** in Larger Print. This collection begins with 3 FREE books and 2 FREE gifts (gifts valued at approx. $20.00 retail) in the first shipment, along with the other first 4 books from the collection! If I do not cancel, I will receive 8 monthly shipments until I have the entire 51-book Montana Mavericks collection. I will receive 2 or 3 FREE books in each shipment and I will pay just $4.99 US/ $5.89 CDN for each of the other four books in each shipment, plus $2.99 for shipping and handling per shipment.*If I decide to keep the entire collection, I'll have paid for only 32 books, because 19 books are FREE! I understand that accepting the 3 free books and gifts places me under no obligation to buy anything. I can always return a shipment and cancel at any time. My free books and gifts are mine to keep no matter what I decide.

263 HCN 2404   463 HCN 2404

Name	(PLEASE PRINT)	
Address		Apt. #
City	State/Prov.	Zip/Postal Code

Signature (if under 18, a parent or guardian must sign)

Mail to the **Reader Service:**

IN U.S.A.: P.O. Box 1867, Buffalo, NY 14240-1867
IN CANADA: P.O. Box 609, Fort Erie, Ontario L2A 5X3